Musings from Yesteryear

Also by Sheenah Freitas

ZINCIAN LEGEND TRILOGY
The Chosen (Book 1)
The Number (Book 2)

MUSINGS
from
YESTERYEAR

a short story collection
Special Edition Copy

Sheenah Freitas

Text copyright © 2012 Sheenah Freitas
Photography copyright © 2016 Sheenah Freitas

All rights reserved. Published by Paper Crane Books.

First Paper Crane Books paperback edition: May 2012
Second Paper Crane Books paperback edition: January 2014
Third Paper Crane Books paperback edition: August 2016

ISBN: 978-0615648071

Table of Contents

Acknowledgements

I'd like to thank Susan for providing such a fantastic title for this anthology. She's a fantastic blogger (and author) and such a great advocate for indie authors. You can learn more about her by visiting her website:
http://mistressofthedarkpath.wordpress.com/

I'd also like to thank the Cornerites just for being awesome. Rhonda, you've provided such a fantastic resource for all writers. I don't think you can be thanked enough for your hard efforts.

For Mr. Wagner,

For teaching me the magic of brevity. Without it, this collection wouldn't be possible.

Introduction

This is a different kind of short story and flash fiction collection. The stories presented in this collection aren't put together by subject or topic and yet there is a reason why they're presented together. These stories were written during the course of my teenage years from when I was 14 all the way up until the end of my teen years. I decided to take the liberty of not polishing them up and instead, presenting them as I deemed them finished. The only editing I have done to them is minor punctuation and spelling for the sole purpose of making the thought clearer.

Most writers would look upon their earlier works and cringe. Some might even burn their work or place it in a drawer, never to be seen again. But, though some of my earlier works might be cringe inducing, I'm still willing to let everyone see the diversity of my writing. I think with each new writing project, you learn something and you grow. And I know that if I hadn't written these stories, there's no way I would have been able to finish a novel, let alone, two.

I'll be presenting my own notes and reflections before each story, on the left hand side.

This special edition copy contains bonus stories that weren't included in the ebook version, including a story I plan on novelizing.

So, I hope you enjoy the stories presented in this collection. I know I enjoyed writing them.

—Sheenah Freitas

The Little Matchstick Girl has always been one of my favorite tales by Hans Christian Anderson. Before fairy tale retellings became the popular thing to do, I had decided to put my own spin on the tale. I wanted it to be very much like the original (there's just something about those matches that's irreplaceable), but I wanted the girl to live. So I took a stab at it. There are some problems with this story, but I think it's salvageable if I ever wanted to polish it up.

This story so happened to win third place in a writing contest my school was holding.

The Gift

My stepfather had thrown me out in the middle of the street. He had been getting more frustrated when my mother died. I never saw him cry as much as I did the night she died; it made me realize how much he really did love her, though he never showed it. In his frustration, he told me it was my fault for letting her die. My fault. But I had known it wasn't true; she died from a lost battle with pneumonia. Greg, my stepfather, had promised us before that he'd take care of us and that if my mother would marry him, we wouldn't have to worry about anything.

It seemed like a fairy tale when they got married. For a while, we really didn't have to worry about anything. Then my grandmother came to live with us. She was sick at the time, but we were soon able to revive her. Though we weren't a middle class family we were able to get what we needed, even with the four of us. But, fairy tales never really have a happy ending. I had to learn that the hard way. When Greg got laid off, we hoped and hoped that they'd call him back. We were wrong.

All of us ended up working because Greg's new job wasn't paying enough. I ended up having to sell matches to bring in my end of the stick. A blizzard came in earlier this year, getting my grandmother sick again. No cure in the world could save her, and she eventually died. Greg had a heart when he had a decent paying job. My mother went to him for comfort, but he turned a cold shoulder, putting all of his time and effort into getting more money. We both told him that even though we were poor, there was still something we were rich in: love. But he laughed at us. "What can love buy in this materialistic world? Without money, you're nothing. And when you're nothing, you're better off dead," he told us.

Mom got sick shortly after that. She didn't die because of me. I had tried my best to bring in some sort of money for us. I was working at least three jobs. Because I wasn't yet 16, I couldn't do much of anything. But, mom didn't just die of a virus. My mom died from a broken heart. It almost seemed like Greg had forgotten what love was until she died. So now, it was my fault. What a joke.

My feet were bare, and the snow came up to the top of my ankles. I couldn't see myself, but I had a feeling that the cold wind had turned my nose and cheeks rosy. I had only been out for a couple of minutes, and already, I was starting to feel numb from the cold. Taking the bag of matches with me, I went to the little booth where I always sat, right in the middle of the shopping district.

Nobody noticed me that day. It was a couple of days before Christmas and everyone was trying to finish their holiday shopping. The wind had started to pick up, and now, I was more aware of my breath in the cold. I shivered, and shook my hands and tried to warm up my arms. I winced suddenly, forgetting the fresh bruises Greg had given me. Since my mom died, he's been letting out his frustrations on me. I've become his human punching bag, not to mention I seem to be doing everything wrong. Whatever happened to the sweet Greg I once knew that was going to protect me from every demon in this world? I suppose he was showing his real face now.

"Box of matches for $2!" I cried. The wind must have carried my voice to a faraway land because nobody even acknowledged that someone had yelled. It didn't matter though, I had other things to sell besides matches. Greg recently got a part time job as a baker, and every now and then he'd bring home a huge box of cookies and mini cakes. He told me once before to never eat any of it because he put me in charge of selling them on the streets. I thought I could get away with it, but Greg had found out and gave me the beating of a lifetime.

I had decided earlier to buy some tins to put the cookies and mini cakes in. It took a while to earn, but when I found some on sale,

I bought them immediately. People seem to notice things more if it's in something pretty. I sifted through my bag of matches, and finally found the tins. I set them out, and with my numb hand, grabbed the sign that advertised I was selling cookies and set it out on the booth. I then placed the tins on the booth in a caring fashion, trying my hardest to imitate the surrounding display windows.

This imitation gave way to a few acknowledgments, but still nobody bought any. I truly wanted to light a match and burn something to get warm. My thin sweater wasn't insulating me and my whole body had turned numb. I didn't know what to do. If I lit a match now, it'd mean getting beat later. But was it my destiny to freeze to death?

The decision was a tough call. I couldn't, no I wouldn't, leave without having at least one dollar to show for my hard work. If I went home with nothing, I was almost positive that Greg would be so infuriated with me, he may almost kill me. That was a scenario I wanted to avoid at all costs. There just had to be someone who needed matches or cookies, wasn't there?

The day wore on, and the district started to thin out more and more. Nobody had bought anything off of me. They say the Christmas season is supposed to bring out the good in people. Well, all I see is the bad. They yell and scream, and mothers turn into hideous beasts, all lined up in front of stores in the wee hours of the morning when it's still dark trying to be the first to get to the sale. There wasn't a soul out there that even took a look at people like me, people who may need some sort of help. Sure, we have holiday baskets and the Salvation Army will do something for us, but is it really from the goodness of the people's hearts, or is it just out of tradition and a good reputation? It's hard these days to tell which people are pure of their intentions and which aren't anymore.

Snow started to fall lightly and gradually fell harder and harder. It chilled me even more when the first flake fell on my already numb nose. I didn't realize it was snowing until I woke up from my daydream state. A Christmas like the ones that they show in the TV shows I saw in the electronics display window would be great. Everyone greeting each other, hugging, and helping. That's the kind of Christmas I wanted. But, what I really wanted was for my family to be a family again. Greg when he was carefree, my mom, and my grandma. We'd be laughing and singing, and nothing, not even the cold, would break our spirit.

Of all times for a blizzard to start, it had to start now. I tried so hard to not light a match, but I just couldn't help it. Greg would have called me weak. With a trembling hand, I lit a match. Its warmth quickly enveloped me and I suddenly felt another source of heat from behind me. I looked and there was a fireplace with a big green chair that looked like it would engulf me if I sat in it. As I started to wonder where it came from, the sudden gust of wind blew out my match and with it, the fireplace.

With it gone, I suddenly felt delirious. Maybe I had been in the cold for too long and was now starting to see things. It could have been possible; I was never informed of my family's past medical history. But, I suddenly longed for that fireplace. Before I knew it, the matches had become a drug to me, and I kept lighting them, one by one.

With each new match that I lit, new visions came before me: a feast, a Christmas tree, presents, and a bed that looked like it was bigger than the little house me and Greg were staying in.

I suddenly grew tired and fell onto the bed. In an instant, everything turned to black.

The smell of bacon and eggs woke me up when I finally came to again. I sat up and a large blanket fell off of me. Surprised, I looked at my surroundings. Maybe those matches were magic matches and transported me to some faraway place. The door knocked. "Come in," I answered awkwardly.

A beautiful girl came in. She had golden hair that was curled at the ends, like a doll. Her smile was delicate and well-practiced along with her curtsy. "Feeling better?" she asked. It took me a minute to get out of my head that this girl really was a doll. The girl's voice was just as sweet as she looked.

"Yeah," I managed to stammer after getting over my immediate shock. "Where am I?"

She stifled a giggle. "My house." So this huge mansion of a room was part of her house. I quickly inferred that the rest of the house had to be full of rooms like this, meaning I was in the home of someone whose world was his oyster. The girl clapped her hands, and in an instant a butler appeared with a breakfast tray. I noted that there was indeed bacon and eggs on there and even blueberry pancakes. "After you're done eating, we'll take you home. We were trying to find an ID on you, but it seems you had none. I'm sure your parents are worried."

I froze for a second. The girl really seemed to be genuine of her feelings. After all, she could have just left me out there in the cold and let me die. "Not parents, parent," I corrected gently. "Stepfather to be exact," I added bitterly. The girl must not have heard the bitterness in my voice because she didn't seem concerned, or maybe she decided to brush it off. Either way, she apologized for her own assumption.

"I have something for you!" the girl chirped. She whisked away leaving me with the butler. I said nothing, eating quietly. It's hard to control yourself when you've been deprived of food, or at least home cooked food, for so long. I wanted to act like one of those beggars that gulped all of their food in one bite. Though I was fairly close to being one of those beggars, I still controlled myself because I was in the presence of first class.

The girl returned with a nice size box. There was shiny red wrapping paper covering it with a lush green ribbon. She almost seemed like she was glowing when she handed it to me, so proud that she was giving me something. I took it graciously and carefully opened it. The wrapping paper was so pretty that I was disappointed when I had to tear it. Inside, was a delicately knit blue sweater. The girl didn't know it, but blue was my favorite color. "But, you don't even know me. Why?" I asked.

"Sara, is that reason enough to not get you something?" she asked.

I took my hand and felt the soft fabric of the sweater. It took me a minute to register that she had called my name. "How did you know my name? I don't know you."

"My mom's an angel," she simply said before kissing me lightly on the forehead. "Nothing but good will come to you on behalf of your mom and grandmother's wishes."

I didn't know what to say or do. In the split second that it took to blink my eyes, I found myself lying in the snow by my booth. I heaved myself up and found that I was wearing the blue sweater that the little girl had given me. Tears formed in my eyes, and people stared at me as I started to cry.

"Sara! Sara!" a familiar voice called. I looked in the direction of the voice and Greg came running over to me. A flicker of fear swept through my body as I thought of him beating me again, but instead he came over and wrapped me in a warm embrace. "I thought I lost you..." he said. It was at that moment that I realized the pain and fear that I had lived through for the past few months were over. Something had happened and now everything was for the best now. I had guardian angels watching over me. Up there, in heaven. This Christmas Eve was going to be the best day I've had for a long while, and Christmas would be even better.

As I look back at that time in my life, I realize now that each day was better than the last. If there's something that I learned on that day, it's that fairy tales do have happy endings. I'm sure of it now. No, I'm positive.

This particular short story is the result of me trying to write a short story for a geometry project. The rules of the project were to incorporate geometry terminology, which is why these two characters sound so ridiculously nerdy. I couldn't finish this in time, so I believe I ended up doing a basic, "This box is a cube" type of book. I don't remember when I finished writing this story or when I even went through to edit out the terrible backstory that I gave poor Summer, but I'm glad I had the sense to go back through and fix it when I did.

Summer

Josh stared blankly at the dark-colored liquid in the cream-colored mug. The day was warm with a light breeze. He brushed away the soft, blond bangs that fell into his face. As people passed idly by he would occasionally look up and down the sidewalk. The outdoor coffee shop attracted many customers, especially the young college students within the area.

"Hey! There you are!" a female voice yelled out. The chirpy woman smiled brightly at him as she sat down across from him. She eyed him slyly and gave a mischievous smirk. "Know any biconditional statements?"

Josh chuckled lightly, humored by her childishness. "An if-and-only-if statement? How about ..." He leaned in closer as if he were going to spill secret information on the government. Summer leaned in until the two's foreheads nearly touched. "If and only if we leave right now we'll make it on time to the meeting," Josh replied. He watched as she sluggishly leaned back in her chair and wrinkled her nose. She was his childhood friend, always there for him; when it was time to decide on a college, they naturally had to go to the same one. It was nice, sitting there in the warmth of the sun, enjoying some nerd humor.

"That's not how it should be used, but I suppose I'll let you slide with that one," Summer said, standing up hastily. She fished out $1.50 from her purse and immediately slammed it on the table. "That's for your coffee."

"Punctual as always." He playfully bowed down to her and enjoyed hearing her laughter. She was named after the season and for good reason. Everything about her reminded people of summer.

There were times when he played dumb to get her to teach him something about their class. He loved it when she got irritated from trying to pound something into his brain that was just so simple. Before he knew it, the unsolicited bliss of first love blossomed. The love was one-sided but it didn't bother him, just as long as he could be with her.

She gave a quick curtsy before grabbing him by the hand. "Come on!" Summer began to drag Josh out of the coffee shop.

"This is the opposite way!"

"I know. I forgot my sketches for the building. Besides, the van's in front of the building."

Josh promptly stopped, pulling Summer back. She looked wildly at him, but as he began to search her hazel eyes, she diverted all eye contact like a misbehaved dog. "Do you mean to tell me..."

"Yes..."

"How could you forget? I swear, you're going to cause us to be late one day," he sighed.

"I know where they are, so it'll take a couple of minutes tops." She stuck out her tongue childishly before abruptly turning around and jogging the rest of the short distance to the apartment building. Josh smiled lightly at her as he watched her disappear into the building. Whistling, he walked to the van and used the spare key to open the wine-colored vehicle. Summer was often forgetful, thus she insisted he have a spare.

As he started the van, the light pat of her feet announced her arrival. She burst in the van, frowning at Josh at first, shrugged, and began situating her sketches. "This is *my* van, ya know."

"I know, I know. Bit of a habit I guess." Josh glanced at her as he shifted the van into drive.

"I know." Summer smiled softly at him before placing her head against the window. She stared out listlessly at the road as he began to drive. Parallel lines kept coming and stopping at exact intervals, on what seemed like a never ending, asphalt covered plane. In a matter of moments she started to continuously move her right leg and began to chew on one of her nails.

Making a quick lane change, Josh caught a glimpse of her. He knew the ritual well. From her first spelling bee, to her last SAT, she never changed her habit. She may look twenty-two, but her personality remained unchanged since she was ten. When the world changed, he changed with it. But Summer stayed true to herself and reminded Josh to do the same.

"Nervous I take it?"

Her eyes widened. "Nervous? How could you not be?" she squeaked.

Josh laughed. "Oh, *I'm* nervous. I just don't advertise it."

Summer frowned. "This meeting is vital to our future. If we make one mistake..."

"Look, we'll do fine. It's just an internship."

"EXACTLY!" she panicked, whipping her head around to look at him. He was silent; a steady rock in her hectic life. Josh was always there to tell her to have fun, he was always there to support her, and he was always there when things went bad.

He reached out and took one of her hands. "It'll be all right. I promise." He turned and smiled lightly at her.

"Thank you," she uttered softly. In that split second, Summer knew he would always be there for her, just like she would be there for him. It was small, but it was there. The unsolicited bliss of first love had blossomed in her heart.

I had this strange sentence pop into my head out of the blue: "My husband died yesterday and yet I feel no remorse or sadness." And that's how this short story came about. I wanted to know what kind of a wife would say that. How long have they been married? Was she not happy? Was he not devoted enough? Or is she just so shocked from the sudden loss that she feels numb?

Until Death Do Us Part

My husband died yesterday and yet I feel no remorse or sadness. I feel nothing, not even the gentle wind on my face. It happened on a regular night. My husband loved to watch whatever the young kids loved to watch these days. I always told him it didn't matter what they watched, but he always insisted upon it because it would help him establish a common ground with our grandchildren. Our *grandchildren!*

For one, we hardly ever see our grandchildren. Since my son was taken away from us by cancer two years ago, our daughter-in-law simply forgot us. Both of us had tried so hard in the beginning to get in contact with them: letters, telephone, e-mail, and friends, but nothing worked. What were we then? Dust in the wind?

And as for our *daughter*, she lived in a faraway country across that vast ocean. She hardly dares to come back and visit us. At the time of my husband's death, she was currently on a business meeting in the Orients, leaving her daughter out and about doing only heaven knows what. Our *daughter* has no husband; they divorced only two years after their marriage—a typical lasting marriage these days, or so I hear.

So as you see, with our estranged *daughter* and daughter-in-law, we never had a relationship with our grandchildren. I often thought of the two of us as being the old couple without any children. Or perhaps the tragic couple who just lost their only child in war. Either way, our family line ends with us.

My husband died suddenly and painlessly. An aneurism. I found him there while waking up due to a sudden chill in the air. I couldn't go back to sleep; it was unusual for me. I was making my way into the kitchen for a glass of water when I found him sitting there in his favorite chair, propped in front of the television. Seeing his bald head poking out from the chair, I changed my direction and headed toward him instead. I'm not sure why, but I was overcome with a sudden heaviness in my chest and as I placed my hand on his shoulder, I knew. For the first time in my old age, he felt cold. The world had gotten colder since I had gotten older, but he—he never did! He was an internal flame, always lighting up the room and warming me with his radiance.

Though I knew, I couldn't help myself. I had always believed that you could see a person's soul through their eyes. My husband always had the most enchanting and purest soul you could ever find. But that night his eyes were lifeless. Listless.

I didn't scream. I didn't cry. I didn't say his name. He was gone. I simply turned away from him and calmly called 911.

All neighbors are nosy. It's a fact. You get a few flashing lights and maybe a siren, and they all come out of their homes like aggravated bees coming out of a hive. It doesn't matter what the time is, they'll be there buzzing. And because neighbors are nosy and tend to gossip, the entire neighborhood knew of my husband's death by morning. Oh, it was queer to know that they knew about his death and didn't even express their condolences. It was even hurtful. They always came running to him when they had a problem or a question or they wanted to borrow something. So where were they now? I swear, people these days don't show the same respect they used to.

"Excuse me," I heard a voice call out. I looked around, startled that someone was in the house with me. I'm very immaculate about things—especially when it comes to locking up the house. After our son died, I've always made sure that the doors were locked. It was worse then; I check them only every few hours now.

A young girl was standing in the hallway with her hair in pigtails. She was so small, so innocent. She looked to be about eight, though she might have been younger. Though I had never seen this girl before, I felt like I had met her and even known her from some long ago time.

"Excuse me," she said again. Her voice was patient and lilting.

"How'd you get in here little girl?" I swiftly interrogated.

"The front door."

"Liar." I glared at her.

Her face was troubled. "It's true!" she pleaded. "Just look at the door!" She pointed toward the door.

I knew she was wrong. I had just checked that door a few minutes before. It was bolted shut. Still…I stole a glance toward the door. It was wide open. The girl looked at me smugly. I stared at her. I didn't like seeing her haughty smile; it made me even more sure that I knew her from somewhere before.

"Who are you?" I asked roughly.

Her eyes fell. "I'm sorry." Her statement threw me off. I looked about for something to say, but nothing came to mind. "I'm sorry," she said again a bit louder when I didn't answer.

I quickly recollected my thoughts. "I'm not deaf little girl. Why are you sorry?" I spat. Since my daughter left, I had never lost my patience to anybody. Never. So how was this little girl, this sweet little girl, able to get under my skin? She hadn't done anything wrong except mysteriously break into my house. Weren't her parents worried about where she was right now?

She looked around the room, as if the answer would lie in an inanimate object. Once her eyes had made a complete orbit of the room, she looked back at me and sighed. The girl sucked in a deep breath, scrunched up her face, placed her hands on her hips and leaned toward me.

"I'm not little! I'm quite big, thank you." Her bottom lip jutted out. "Besides…didn't your husband die or somethin'?"

Yes, my husband was dead. It wasn't any secret or anything like that. I somehow wandered over to the very chair he had died in, and rocked back and forth, lost in thought. When I looked back, the girl was gone. The door was exactly how I had remembered it before she came: closed and locked tight. Was that girl still in the house? Surely I would have heard her leave…But wouldn't I have heard her come in as well?

I sank back down into the chair and sighed. Today had been dreadfully long. And terribly lonely.

There was a time when I was terribly lonely in elementary school. My hair was usually fixed up in pigtails, just like that little girl, and a boy decided to make fun of me. I was always reserved and never had any real friends. That boy had always heckled and taunted me; it irritated me every day. And then one day, he stopped completely. It was as if I didn't exist in his world. I was elated. My world was at peace. And then I began longing for him. He had been the only one to acknowledge my existence. That longing and despair slowly turned to love and gratitude. He died in war—our town's first casualty. We were engaged at that time and I had sunk into terrible loneliness. The only one who had been able to take me out of those deep waters—if only a little—was my husband. And he was taken from me just like my love.

In our old age, my husband had been my only interaction. And yet, I still couldn't cry for him. Maybe it wasn't because I couldn't. Maybe I just wouldn't.

The clock chimed six o' clock, waking me out of my reverie. Everything within the house was silent. It was late and I was tired and hungry. I decided to head to the kitchen and reheat some leftovers for supper.

"Turkey? I thought that stuff was for Thanksgivin' Day," a woman said as I entered the kitchen. She was standing in front of the refrigerator, the door wide open, and staring at the content of food within the Tupperware she was holding. "Can't believe you're eatin' it myself... Wouldn't you much prefer somethin' else?" She turned and looked at me. Her hair was worn short, just like mine when I was seventeen; she couldn't have been much older than that.

"Who are you?" I demanded while taking a peek at the back door. It was wide open. I hadn't checked this lock in a while, but I had a hunch that it had been locked just like the front door.

The woman frowned and glared. "Who are *you*?" I remembered seeing this woman before, but I couldn't put a name to her.

"Now you listen here," I began. She closed the refrigerator door and made her way to the counter. Slowly, she began opening the drawers one by one. She stopped when she reached the silverware and stared aimlessly at the knives.

"He died alone. We all die alone in a sense, you know?" Her eyes were glued to the knives.

I took a step back. "What are you talkin' about?" I whispered.

"We all die alone. Your husband, especially. He was alone in death."

"No he wasn't," I replied curtly. "*I* was there for him. *He* left *me*."

"Are you sure?" she whispered.

My temper flared. "Of course I'm sure! Now answer my question! *Who are you?!*" I screamed.

The woman looked at me then. Her eyes were melancholy, shining with tears that she was holding back. "You don't remember? You don't remember me? Have you really lost me?" she choked. I continued to stare at her until she walked away out into the living room. I heard the front door open, then shut. I peeked into the living room; she was gone. I turned back toward the kitchen. The drawer was still open. The door, however, was shut and locked.

I walked toward the drawer and shut it. My hands were trembling with rage and fear. Her words crawled under my skin. When I was younger, I never really liked turkey either. I'd tolerate it for Thanksgiving Day, but that was the only time when I'd eat it without complaints—much complaints, anyway. I had appreciated the knock-out bird only when I got older. Maybe we were more alike than I had first thought, she and I. It irritated me.

But what angered me the most of all was what she said about my husband. My husband died alone? That wasn't right at all. *I* would be the one to die all alone. So why did my stomach fall and my heart ache every time I thought about him dying alone?

My evening continued quietly. I had decided to eat the turkey cold, finishing up whatever was left in the Tupperware. I decided to take a shower. Maybe that was what I needed to clear my mind of the day's events. Then I would be able to grieve.

I let the warm water run in the tub while I set out my toothbrush and toothpaste on the sink counter. My pajamas were neatly folded adjacent to them. Despite the heat the water was emitting, a cold chill ran down my spine.

"Do you remember me now?" I heard the woman ask.

I turned to look at her. The little girl was standing beside her with a deep overwhelming sadness in her eyes. How did they get around so silently? Where were their parents?

"No," I said, annoyed.

The woman frowned. "That's interestin'," she murmured to herself.

"Go bother someone else," I snapped.

I turned around, closed my eyes, and sucked in a deep breath. I exhaled slowly and began counting to ten. Hopefully by then she would be gone. I made it to four when I felt two hands around my neck. The woman was strangling me! Where was the little girl? My eyes flew open and I found myself staring in the mirror. But I wasn't staring at an image of me with a woman strangling myself. I found myself staring at me—me younger. Blood saturated the bath water. My blood. I was there, within the tub, strangling myself because I wasn't dying fast enough. The kitchen knife I had used on myself was discarded somewhere near the tub on the bathroom floor.

Our third child was a miscarriage. It was what had sent me over the edge that day. The day I had died. Alone. My husband would be home within minutes. Our two other children—a daughter and son—were away at school. Only my husband would see this mess. He'd have it cleaned before they came home. My daughter never got over my death; she wanted to blame someone, and decided to blame her father. When she became an adult, she left and never looked back. My son forgave me and his sister. He loved his father and did eventually die of cancer. His wife hated looking into the eyes of a broken man every time she saw my husband and drifted away.

He died alone from an aneurism at the ripe old age of eighty-eight. Our daughter-in-law found him early in the morning the next day. She had returned to apologize.

I saw him pass. He was old. I was eternally youthful. He smiled at me—waved even—but then frowned. His brow creased when he saw where I was versus where he was going.

Suicide grants you admission into the seventh circle of hell. Within the walls of the seventh circle, I lie within the middle ring, my body gnarled into a thorny bush amongst others like me. I was reliving my own personal hell for eternity.

"Until death do us part," he mouthed before the angels took him away.

I believe this was my first flash fiction. I had never heard of anything less than a short story until my senior year in high school. Mr. Wagner, my creative writing teacher, randomly handed out pictures and we were supposed to write a flash fiction based off them. I vividly remember the picture I was given: A boy, with one of his hands on his head with a horror-struck expression surrounded by his classmates. I had never wrote anything humorous before but decided to take a stab at it here.

Late Again

BZZZT! BZZZT! With a groan I rolled over and hit my alarm clock. The numbers blinking at me read seven forty-five. Seven forty-five? How long was I asleep? With a quick leap, I was out of bed.

Clothes were placed everywhere, papers scattered about. The paper I grabbed was near my socks and I swiftly stuffed it into my bookbag. I raced out of the house like a Nascar driver and didn't slow down once. Street signs, houses, dogs, and lawns all blurred by as I continued my mad sprint to school. It usually took twenty minutes to get to school and another ten to get ready. That made the whole process thirty minutes long. I managed to do it within fifteen today. Fifteen. The number seemed magical.

I wheezed my way into class and slumped in my desk. Sluggishly, I pulled out the slightly crumpled paper and placed it on my desk before looking around the room. The faces, all staring at me quizzically, didn't look familiar. Who were they? I looked at the teacher. Even he wasn't familiar.

I stood immediately, holding my head with one hand, my homework in the other. "Oh no..." I blurted out loud as the eight o' clock bell rang clear. I took a glance at the paper in my hand. It was dated from last week. Wrong homework. Wrong class. Looks like I was late again.

This is absolutely, hands down, one of my favorite works. It's sort of poetic and you really need to read between the lines to figure out what happened. I decided to flex my literary muscle when I crafted this together. (The power of repetition!)

This is another assignment from high school. I was having problems coming up with an idea for this and since the last picture prompt sparked something in me, I went on a quest for pictures and came across this picture of a man silhouetted by a camp fire. It was sort of haunting and beautiful and I couldn't help but ask, "Why does he look so sad? Why is he all alone?" In my quest for answers, this flash fiction came about.

The Camping Trip

The sky started to shine with gold, orange, and red. The forest was quickly darkening. His friends would be back. They always came back. Listlessly, he placed another log into the blazing fire. It roared with life and the sharp snap of the splitting log filled the surrounding wood.

Birds chirped to one another, hidden among leaves, out of sight. The warmth of the blaze kept him from becoming chilled in the light autumn breeze. They would come back. They always came back.

He placed his head against his fist, and looked at the tent facing him. Bobby always slept there. The one next to it was his, and the one next to that was June's. On the other side of Bobby's tent was Mia's, and next to hers was Robert's.

Laughter filled the air. People moved about. Bobby twirled June around and he watched as blonde strands caressed the two. Robert brought the van around. Then ... and then ...

It was their annual camping trip. They would come back. They always came back ... wouldn't they?

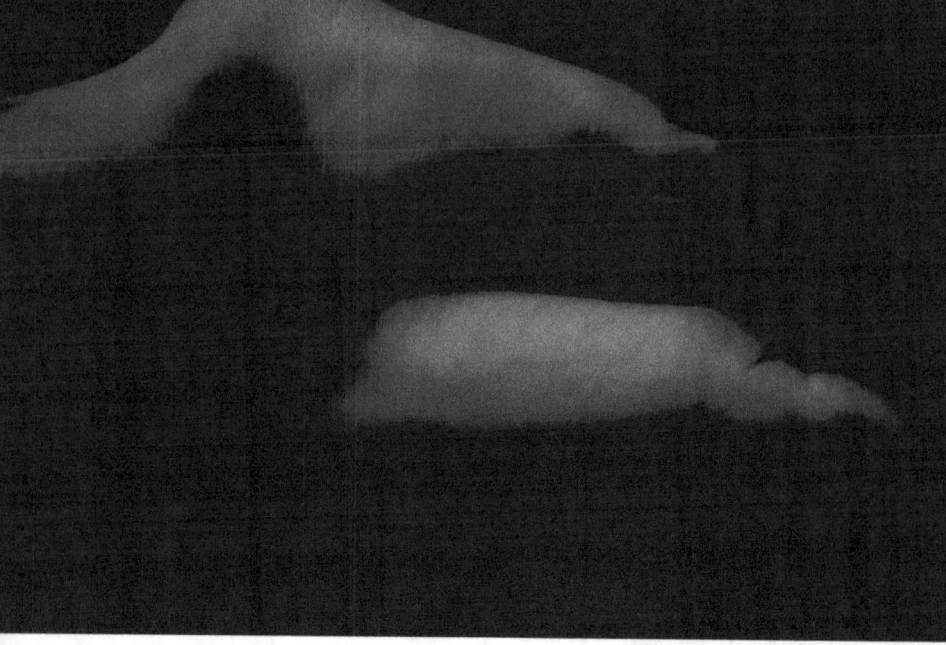

While I was at work one day, the radio decided to play back-to-back songs about cheating. I don't think it was intentional, but it did make my mind go into overdrive and a sentence began creeping into my mind, "But for one night, you made me feel *alive*." I had to do something about it and luckily I was carrying around index cards. And that was the day I crafted a flash fiction on an index card and learned that Mr. Wagner was absolutely right when he said you could fit a flash fiction on an index card. The lesson: Never doubt your teachers.

One Night Only

Your touch elicits a shock through my spine. Our lips suddenly collide, locked in their own battle. I begin to lead the two of us through my apartment. The scrape of the kitchen chairs reach my ears; I am blind, my eyes won't open. My legs know where my room is, they shall take us there safely.

Barely making it through the threshold, I can feel your breath on my neck. The heat lingers there for a while before slowly trailing down my body.

For one night make me feel special. For one night tell me you love me, though both of us know you don't. For one night, take my mind off of my spiraling downwards life.

The two of us move in sync toward my bed. Heavy breathing and gasps permeate the air; I still seem incapable of seeing. I can feel you clinging to me, as if you'd die without me.

When the sun filters through the curtains and hits my face, I know you won't be in bed next to me. I won't know your name and I'll barely remember your face; we may never even see each other again. But for one night, you made me feel *alive*.

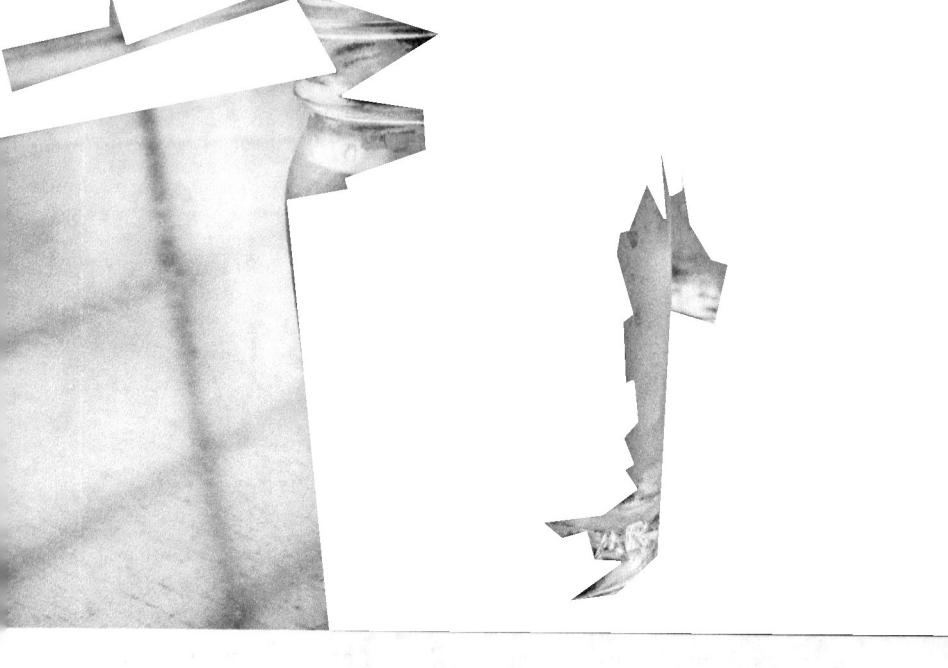

After I finished writing "One Night Only" I began to wonder what the man's perspective of this would be. What was going through his mind that led him to that moment?

For A Moment

Call it fate or destiny, I call it choice. Coincidence. That's what led me at that place and time.

You mistook my drink for yours and when your hand touched mine, a shock ran through my spine. I saw in you everything I saw in me: Loneliness, want, and despair. Time stood still.

Your hand fumbles for your door. The two of us nearly crash into your apartment, our mouths already exploring each other. I keep moving and hitting the kitchen chairs as you lead me to your room.

Barely making it through the threshold, my mouth trails downward, lingering at your neck.

Is this right? I am a person who teaches the future. I am the one married with two beautiful children. I love them.

A sigh escapes your lips, egging me to continue down your body.

For a moment let me do the wrong thing. For a moment take my responsibilities away. For a moment, just let me forget.

The two of us move in sync toward your bed. Heavy breathing and gasps permeate the air. I cling to your body because I feel I'll die if I don't.

When I slip out your apartment, I leave with no regrets. I won't know your name and I'll barely remember your body; we may never even see each other again. But for a moment, you made me feel *real*.

Out of all the things that inspired stories, I'm pretty sure this is up there in the random department. I was outside taking a puppy out when I heard crows. They wouldn't shut up and they were the loudest I have ever heard. And for a split second, I thought, "Is someone going to die?" And that's all it took for me to start developing this story while I tried desperately not to fall on some ice.

Foolish

The pure white snow fell lightly from the heavens. A group of crows shimmered in the moonlight.

I stepped in front of an empty lot in a desolate neighborhood. Leaving the engine running in my black Ferrari, I cautiously stepped out into the frosty evening. The snow crunched under my footsteps, the wind nipped my face. I rubbed my arms. A crow flew overhead to join the flock in the tree, laughing as it rushed past me.

Out of the shadows a man stepped into the pool of light cast by the lone lamp post. I greeted him as nicely as I could. The crows rustled in the trees.

I had rehearsed everything I wanted to say to this man. I made no threats, I stated very precisely what I wanted in a calm manner, despite the circumstances. He appeared to understand. His face was hidden in shadow, much like the night we had met.

Finished with what I needed to say, I waited. There appeared to be nothing he wanted to say. Who knew that something as simple as shaking his hand in farewell, a sign that I saw him as my equal—not my rival, would undo me? I had no time to act.

Red stained white like falling rose petals. I fell. The man walked over me and took my wedding band. I heard the door of my Ferrari open and slam shut.

I could hear the crows laugh and jest. Their feathers showered over me. The last image in my mind was of her—my beloved wife. I forgave her.

I was the fool.

When you're in high school, you're being forced to read a lot of books and stories that are just saturated with symbolism and themes. So with this flash fiction, I wanted to incorporate some heavy symbolism and try to recreate that artsy, literary feel. Perhaps I went a bit too far?

Sanctuary

The clock was about to strike midnight. Thunder boomed in the distance. We were moving stealthily across the lawn, making our way toward the lingering wood that surrounded the home. Deep beneath the foliage was our secret place: a place where magic happened.

We paid no heed to the ominous clouds that were swiftly covering the light of the full moon that night. By the time the midnight sun blew out, we were already well inside the fortress of the woods. Voices of the past whispered to us. Fireflies swirled all around us, lighting the way.

Rain began pelting down all around us. Thor banged his mighty hammer down. The two of us froze. Were those the faeries trying to communicate to us?

Mud covered everything. Hades was laughing from across the Styx. Osiris looked on. My friend's hair got caught in a branch and once I and the Fates cut it simultaneously, she fell. Down, down, down, into the river that was too close.

Every year I return to our secret place. Magic still lingers there— if you can find it.

In my quest to find stories I wrote as a teen, I came across this. I had totally forgotten all about it. And because I forgot all about it, it's the roughest story in this collection.

I believe I came across a forum somewhere where the original poster thought it would be fun to have a short story contest. They posted pictures that were to be our prompt or maybe we were supposed to include them in the story. I don't remember if I entered or not, but I vaguely recall going back and reading through the entries which were all enjoyable. The poster said they felt no one hit the core of the theme (whatever the theme was) and therefore didn't pick a winner. Ridiculous, right?

Happy: Straight Ahead

There are many different reasons why people decide to go down the path of suicide. Most feel that they aren't getting enough attention, like they're not wanted. Some do it because life is just too difficult and they just can't cope. Others do it because they're just tired of waiting for everything to end. Why did I decide that it was time to end my life? Simple: love.

Women are evil—have been since the beginning of creation. Just open a Bible to Genesis and you can read that because of woman, men were tempted to go against what we were told and eat from the tree of knowledge. And women have been the fall of many honorable men. Take a look at women like Delilah or even Helen of Troy. Then you have temptresses such as the Sirens and Medusa (who was once beautiful). All of these women are out there trying to win your heart. They'll learn your weaknesses, what makes you vulnerable, and then without any warning—BAM! They'll leave you broken, never to be heard from again.

I found myself staring straight into the face of a child. He looked at me peculiarly, attempting to hide himself with a pink daisy. I blinked. He continued to stare.

The last thing I could clearly recollect was my car breaking down as I drove aimlessly around, searching for that perfect curve to miss and effectively kill myself. Frustrated, I had taken my wanderings on foot. The air was hot and muggy; oppressive. There was a point where everything blurred and the ground met my face. Death had met me after all.

It had never occurred to me that I would find a child staring at me after I had died. But, children die too, right? Still, because I was searching for suicide, I had thought that I would end up in hell, waking up to harpies attacking my disfigured body. Children definitely don't end up in the seventh circle of hell; they're too innocent.

"Hey, Dan! What are you doing over there?" a female voice called.

I froze. So I wasn't dead.

The woman came partially into view and pulled the boy, Dan, close to her body. She leaned down a bit to get a better view of me.

"What did you find, Dan?" she asked the boy. He said nothing. She looked at me again. "Hey mister ... Mister, are you all right?"

My eyes found hers. I'm not sure what she saw there, but she pulled the boy away and whispered something to him. She hurried back over to me.

"Everything will be all right. My name is Julie. Can you hear me?"

I think I nodded. Everything was beginning to become hazy again. It felt like I was underwater, hearing her voice becoming more and more distorted. Even her face was becoming more and more blurred. And then silence. And darkness.

"Hello, there! You gave us quite a scare earlier. We thought you were dead." The woman smiled at me.

I stared at her. I definitely felt stronger than the last time I was conscious.

"Seems like you were just suffering from major heat exhaustion. It's pretty hot out there, so you need to be more careful. The doctor told me to make sure you drink plenty of water. So here," she said, placing a cup of water in my face.

I cringed. I did not need to be nursed back to health by a woman—the enemy, no less. But the woman insisted and even placed a straw in the cup, urging me to drink. I drank reluctantly, only because I was, indeed, quite thirsty.

"So, what were you doing out there?"

"My car broke down," I answered. My voice startled me. It was hoarse and disfigured like a monster.

"I see," Julie said, though I doubt she saw at all. "I'll send Bill out to look for your car. In the meantime, the doctor wants you to stay and rest for a couple of days."

I nodded slowly as I sipped the water. So death was going to have to wait a couple more days. I could tolerate that. Julie smiled at me and left, telling me that if there was anything I needed, anything at all, to not hesitate and ask. I of course answered with the typical, "Of course" response, though nobody really does, do they?

Throughout the day I drifted from the world of the living to an infinite black abyss. When I was in the world of the living, I could hear Julie humming softly somewhere in the house. The sunlight radiated through the window, warming my skin. It was peaceful here. When I was floating in the black abyss, I could hear someone crying. It was frigid. It was terrifying here. A snake slithered up my leg, hissing that everything was okay.

"Your eyesss just haven't adjusted to the darknesss. It'sss a paradise," the snake continued to hiss.

"Let's go," Julie's voice called.

"Go where? I thought I had to rest."

Julie smiled slyly. "As your caretaker, I say that you need to go out."

She grabbed me by the hand and pulled me up. I didn't bother to resist. The boy, Dan, was standing in the kitchen, watching me carefully. He was holding a large picnic basket. Julie took him by the hand and lugged the two of us outside. The clouds were heavy and dark.

"It's going to rain soon," I said.

Julie's only response was a sweet smile. Her grip on my hand tightened as she continued to lead me down the street. The town, I now saw, was tiny, consisting of one main road, and a few side roads. There was, as far as I could tell, one grocery store and an auto repair shop that also doubled as a gasoline station. The houses were run down, but the people looked content. It was the kind of town that should have given up already. But here it was. Still chugging along. Made a person wonder how they could continue to go on.

A drop of rain fell on my nose. Another fell on my arm. Another on the top of my head. My cheek. My finger. Two on my shoulder. And then the heavens ripped open, dousing the three of us.

Julie began laughing and took off her shoes.

"What are you doing?" I yelled at her. The rain was coming down so strong, it was drowning out my voice.

"Take off your shoes!" she ordered. She was already prying the picnic basket away from Dan. Dan quietly took off his shoes and allowed Julie to lead him into the pool of light provided by the light pole. With a soft sigh, I took off my shoes and followed the two. I was hoping that if I humored her a bit, she would listen to reason and allow us to find shelter at her house.

"Doesn't this feel wonderful?" Julie tilted her head back and allowed the rain to wash her face. I had to admit that the rain did feel nice, especially after the oppressive mugginess of the day.

Julie bent down and splashed me with water that was swiftly flooding the ground. To my surprise, Dan jumped into a large puddle, soaking me even more. I kicked some water toward Julie, who teamed up with Dan and attempted to tackle me down into the water. I evaded them, grabbed Julie by the waist and pulled her down to the ground. Our faces were inches from each other. Dan hopped onto my back, allowing me to close the gap between our faces. Our lips brushed against one another for a second before she splashed water into my face. Our laughter rang down the street.

"She'sss the enemy," the snake hissed. The snake continued to slither up my leg. I ignored her and tried to figure out where the crying was coming from.

"She'll leave you, just like *her*."

I walked along the darkness, trying to see through it. The snake had said that if I could see past the darkness, I'd find a paradise. But the further I walked, the more crying I could hear. And screams.

"You belong with me," the snake whispered as she continued her climb up my leg. "Sssstay with me."

"It's not going to be raining today, so we'll have our picnic today!" Julie walked into my room, bringing with her warmth and sunshine.

"Are you going to leave me?" I stared outside the window.

"Like, leave you alone in the field?" I could hear her smile. "No. I'm supposed to be watching over you until you recuperate. Doctor's orders," she chimed.

She managed to pull me out of bed and again led me out of the room. She waited for me patiently in the kitchen while I washed my face. My clothes had been soaked through the previous night, but she had taken them and washed them. I was given clothes to sleep in that had belonged to a certain someone that she did not want to talk about. The clothing felt stiff and scratchy, like it knew it didn't belong to me and how dare I put them on.

Shedding that scratchy skin and replacing it with my newly washed clothes was relieving. When I was suitable to be seen, I walked out and she led the way. Apparently Dan was at his own house, recovering from a slight cold he had retrieved from yesterday. His mother wasn't at all pleased with Julie, but that was to be expected.

We walked along the road that we had walked along before, leaving the town behind. There was a field not too far from the small town—village is more appropriate, now that I think of it—where a section of woods skittered around the edges. Julie promptly walked out into the middle of the field and placed the large picnic basket down. She unearthed a red and white checkered blanket, which "you couldn't have a picnic without" and began unpacking the hearty lunch she had prepared. As she was doing this, I looked out toward the woods and saw a tree house.

"Whose tree house?"

Julie glanced up from her work. "Oh, that old thing? That's my secret base."

I raised an eyebrow. "Aren't you a bit old for secret bases?"

She shrugged. "Perhaps. But I like it. It feels nice that you can make something and call it your own."

I sat down and picked up a sandwich. "What do you do?" I asked as I took a bite.

Julie sighed and sat, glancing dreamily back at her secret base. "I help people."

"Help people . . . like how?"

"With whatever they need. You should know that more than anyone else. I'm helping you, aren't I?"

I shrugged and continued to eat. She sighed and ate silently with me. For a while, we were fine like that. The two of us together, eating on a picnic blanket, staring out at nothing but a vast field lined with forest. And for a silly little instance, I could see the two of us together in a few years. Content. But that's the problem with me—I always fall in love too easily. It's just so simple. I was beginning to see that Julie wasn't the enemy after all. Maybe women weren't the enemy.

"You belong with me," the snake hissed in my head.

I jumped. Julie, startled, looked around.

"What's wrong?"

"The snake!"

"Snake?" She searched the area more closely. "I don't see one."

"In my head! On my leg!" I pulled my pant leg up, but there was no snake.

Julie didn't call me crazy. She didn't even look at me like I was crazy. She simply took my hand and led me toward the trees. For a split second I thought she was going to lead me into the middle of the woods and leave me there, trying to find my way back out. But then I noticed her secret base coming closer into view.

She pulled down a rope ladder and headed up. Without being told, I followed her up. She sat down in a corner, tucking her legs beneath her. I hesitated, but eventually sat down. She took in a shaky breath before she launched into a story. It was eerily similar to mine: about how she had fallen in love and how he had left her. She wanted to die. She had seen the snake, listened to it making promises about a paradise. Just when she felt she was going to give in to the snake's temptation, she found out she was pregnant.

"That snake…it's the devil, you know," Julie whispered. "Don't give in. That's what he wants. He wants you to lure you into the darkness; the darkness isn't paradise—it's hell. And we'll suffer for eternity if we give in."

"The baby…what happened to it?"

"He's growing nicely. He's shy, but sweet. I couldn't afford to take care of him, so I gave him away. The woman's nice enough to let me see him, but she's upset that me, his own biological mother, wasn't thinking the other day and allowed him to get sick."

I stared at her. "Dan's yours?"

"Looks like his father."

My hand reached for her. "Come with me. You and Dan. Let's get away from here."

She smiled. "I belong here. I've found Happy and I'm happy here, believe it or not. You're a sweet man. But you don't belong with me. You've discovered Happy. Now what are you going to do with it?"

Julie left me in her secret base. I watched her climb back down the rope ladder. I could see her make her way toward the picnic blanket and slowly put everything away. As the sun began setting in the distance, Julie danced to the music in her head. She looked up at me from my perch in the tree, smiled and waved. And then she was gone.

My car was ready the next day, thanks to Bill's diligent care. I drove away, afraid to even go back to Julie's house to say goodbye. I was terrified to see her one last time, terrified that I might just drag her out of the house and take her with me.

But Julie was right. I didn't belong with her. I discovered Happy and its secret: the secret to move on. The woman I'm with now will be mine forever, starting tomorrow. What would I have done without Julie? I often find myself thinking that I would've given in to the snake.

I'm driving along a road that I haven't driven along in years. I stop, just before I enter the village. I just need to reassure myself that this place certainly does exist. I make a U-turn and glance in the mirror. The reflection tells me the one thing that I already know: Happy is straight ahead.

I came across this really fun writing exercise once upon a time ago. Basically: you ask someone to give you a random word and number between 100 and 1,000. The number becomes your word count and the word becomes the title to your flash fiction and it must be the last word in your story.

I asked my brother for a word and a number. The number: 101. The word: Poop. Challenge accepted.

Poop

There is that split second moment when you open your eyes where you just know you're going to have a bad day. And it happened to Harry. He didn't know what was going to happen—how could he?—but something terrible was definitely going to happen.

His girlfriend, Fiona, of ten years was sitting at the table. An array of food awaited him. It couldn't be that bad a day, could it? Harry cut into his waffle, savoring the taste.

"I was thinking," Fiona began slowly; her eyes flickered toward him. "We should get married."

He nearly choked. "Poop."

I had my dad give me a word and number for the writing exercise. His word: Dog. Number: 102.

Dog

Duke was my best friend and dog. Unfortunately he had bitten my kid sister. Timidity problems. Duke sat awaiting his sentence; I barricaded him from Pa, glaring down the barrel of the shotgun.

"Move," Pa ordered. "An animal like that needs to be put down. You can't trust him."

"It won't happen again."

"Damn right it won't." *Ka-chick!* "I'm giving you to the count of three. One..."

I stiffened.

"Two..."

Duke bolted toward the house barking. We chased after him.

We found my kid sister choking on a dime. A few minutes later and well...

Pa glanced at Duke. "That's some dog."

The purpose of this story was to help me break out of my shell. The books and stories I've read have never had homosexual couples in them and I've never went out of my way to acquire any stories that have. So in terms of writing characters that would be homosexual, I was very uncomfortable with it and tended to avoid it (also helped that none of my characters were homosexual themselves).

There was this anime graphic designer that I looked up to. She had great work and she closed down her original site and decided she wanted to specialize in BL (boy love) anime/manga graphics. I'm not a fan of BL, but I still went to the new site every now and then because, again, I liked her work. And she decided to host a BL/Yaoi contest. There were three categories, I think, and one was for writing. And I thought to myself that this would be the perfect time to really challenge myself and tackle a subject I wasn't comfortable with.

I had a difficult time coming up with a plot line for this and originally wanted it to be about AIDS. But when I realized that my main character wasn't homosexual at all (or so he thought), everything just naturally fell into place.

My Own Treasure

"What do you want?" Travis sighed into the phone.

There was a moment of hesitation. "A baby," Rebecca answered. Her voice wavered.

Travis glanced at the sable-haired god sleeping naked in bed.

"You know I can't do that," he whispered hastily.

"All of those promises you made to me before...what were they? Lies?"

He ran a hand through his tousled hair. "I thought it was understood that those promises don't apply anymore."

"Just think about it," she whispered huskily before terminating the call.

Travis listened to the dial tone until the operator began giving strict instructions to hang up and try again. He sighed and stared out the window. The morning sun was just peeking over the looming skyscrapers; people were already running about. Horns honked from far away; trains rumbled in the distance. This city truly was the city that never slept. When he turned, a pair of chestnut orbs stared back at him. The god had shifted a blanket over himself, covering up his perfect anatomy.

"What did Rebecca want?" he asked. He half-turned toward the nightstand near him and succeeded in grabbing a pack of cigarettes.

"How did you know?" Travis asked. He watched his god intently; the god tapped the bottom of the pack succinctly until a cigarette emerged.

He tossed the rest of the pack on the nightstand and searched for his lighter. Lighting up, he muttered, "Who else would call this fucking early?" The fire illuminated his pale face. He blew out the smoke with a soft gust, making a perfect 'O' with his mouth. "So what did she want?" His gaze drifted back to Travis.

Travis couldn't tear his gaze away from him. His eyes traced the contours of his god's lips, remembering how very soft they felt and what they had done to him last night…

"She wants a baby," Travis said slowly, trying to remain calm.

The god laughed as he took another puff. "Figures. Her fucking biological clock is ticking away."

"Don't say that," Travis defended feebly. He walked toward the bed without thinking.

Chestnut orbs watched his journey carefully.

"Just give her what she wants. Then maybe she'll stop fucking calling so god damn early."

"You know I can't," Travis whispered tenderly. He sat on the edge of the bed, staring intently at the man.

The god rolled his eyes and exhaled more smoke.

"I'm not fucking God or Jesus or whoever the fuck you think I am. I am Seth." He took another long drag and exhaled. "Would God smoke this poisonous shit?" He tossed the pack of cigarettes toward Travis. "Would Jesus fucking talk the way I do? Hell, would he even *fuck* another man?"

Travis lay beside Seth, stroking his hair out of his perfect chestnut eyes. Seth frowned at him, but nonetheless allowed it.

"You know it is speculated that Jesus might have been homosexual," Travis said seriously. Seth pushed his hand away. A grin stretched across Travis' face.

"Well then, call me fucking Jesus," Seth muttered as he took one last puff of his cigarette. He extinguished it quickly, exhaled, and got up. "I have an interview today. Think about Rebecca. You owe her fucking big time."

Travis watched him disappear into the bathroom and sighed. As much as he hated to admit it, he did owe her. At least this much. During the course of their relationship, she had always been so selfless, seeking to obtain whatever it was he wanted and giving it to him. There was no end to her giving. She gave and gave and gave, even if it meant rearranging her life—or destroying it. What was so wrong with giving her this one little thing? Did she have no right to be selfish at least this once?

He shifted to his side to watch the city awaken from the window. It had been an ordinary day then. He had been staring out the window too that morning when his life, which had been carved in stone, suddenly changed. The designer, by some sort of sick sense of humor, had decided to change drastic details in his carving at the last second—so much so, that Travis couldn't even tell what the outcome would be anymore.

The scenery had been different. Then, he had been staring out into a lush backyard… Cigarettes didn't permeate the air; a sweet floral scent washed over him. Silky, dark brown hair curtained his face. Rebecca's matching eyes greeted him tenderly. She placed a soft, warm kiss on his lips and smiled lovingly at him.

"Morning, handsome," she whispered in his ear.

Travis turned to stare at her. She wasn't perfect, but for him—at that moment—she was the only one he needed. Did heaven look this pleasant in the morning? His eyes drifted down toward her body, stopping momentarily at the strap of her silky nightgown which had begun to fall down her shoulder.

"Morning, gorgeous," he whispered back. His hands traced up her arms and carefully pulled the strap back in place. Were people supposed to be so soft?

She blushed and looked away from him.

"Have you finished your wedding vows?" She plucked at some lint on the blanket.

It was his turn to look away. "Er…no," he said. He managed to glance at her.

Rebecca appeared to be calm. She shrugged. "That's fine. Even just saying, 'I love you,' would be enough for me." Her dark brown eyes focused on him. "Travis, I know you have trouble saying how you feel. We didn't have to write our own vows. We can just say the traditional vows."

Travis shook his head. "I want you to know how much I love you."

With one swift movement, Rebecca found herself pinned beneath him. She giggled.

"Surely you can wait until the end of the week?"

Travis sighed in defeat and let her go. She kissed him on the cheek and hopped out of bed. She half-spun around and winked at him before marching off toward the bathroom. He plopped back down on the bed, staring absently at the ceiling. He hadn't even thought of the wedding vows until now. Exactly what *was* he going to say when the time came? His mind searched for words when her face came back into view.

She smiled warmly again, putting heaven to shame. "Don't think about it too much. You have the day off today. Why not take your mind off of it? It'll come to you," she promised.

He pulled her down for a deep kiss. "Well, since you promised..."

"It'll work." She smiled and placed another kiss on his lips. "I'll see you later!"

He smiled back at her. Life had been simple. He could see the goal: their own home, two children, a dog. On holidays, their parents would come over; the mothers would both exclaim over his wife's amazing culinary skills—her mother would boast she had taught her daughter everything she knew. They would grow old together, content with each other's company. He could see the small squabbles, and he could see they would get through each and every one. If only he had known, he may never would have gone to the diner that day.

As fate would have it—because how else could he describe the pull that led him that day?—a few hours after Rebecca left, Travis left the house. A tablet of paper, a pen, and a wallet were the only things he took with him. He drove aimlessly around, unsure of what exactly it was he was looking for.

The little diner was hidden between the shadows of the looming structures it was stashed between. With a retro theme and few cars, the place looked like the perfect place his muse would appear to him.

Travis sat at the counter and ordered a sandwich and a large Coke. The waitress didn't appear to be interested in whatever it was he was writing, and he felt an alarming amount of gratitude toward her. Panic didn't start creeping in until the sandwich was finished, the Coke emptied, and the apple pie he ordered earlier had nearly disappeared. The pen drummed an irregular fast beat on the pristine counter as he tried to collect his thoughts. Exactly how *did* he feel about Rebecca?

The image of her filled his mind, completely overwhelming him. Her smile, her eyes, her hair, her legs, her arms. She was everything to him, and he—he knew all too well—was her universe. So why did an unsettling feeling wash over him as he thought about their life together? Travis chanted to himself that he was just nervous about the wedding; the commitment was daunting and commitment was never his thing until she came along.

"What are you writing about?" a man questioned.

Travis turned, surprised to see someone sitting next to him. The man's black hair was greasy and came falling to his shoulders; multiple piercings decorated both of his ears, one piercing above an eyebrow, and one on his nose; his entire attire was black and silver; worst of all, he smelled like nothing but smoke. Travis studied him warily; this man was the very essence of trouble.

"My wedding vows," he muttered quickly.

"What was that?" the man asked, leaning in to hear.

"My wedding vows," Travis answered louder.

The man, much to the detest of Travis, peered over to look at the tablet of paper. He frowned.

"There's nothing fucking there, man," he said. "Did you just start or something?"

"About an hour ago," the waitress offered before Travis could say anything. She winked and smiled at him before taking away his empty dessert plate. His mouth hung open in silent protest.

The man let out a low whistle. "Don't like her? It's not like she's forcing you to fucking marry her, is she? What? Does she have a fucking gun up to your head?"

Travis recovered from the waitress' betrayal. Not even during college or high school had he heard 'fuck' used in such a small amount of time.

"What?" The man glared at him. "Is there something on my fucking face?"

Travis frowned and turned back toward his paper. "No. But there is something wrong with your language."

"What's fucking wrong with my fucking language?"

He eyed him carefully. "That right there. It's atrocious."

The man smiled. "Huh," he breathed. "Well, don't let my shitty language bother you."

Travis shook his head in disbelief. Was this guy for real?

"My name's Seth, by the way," the man offered.

"Travis," Travis replied reflexively. He kicked himself mentally.

Appearing appeased, Seth turned and made his order. He stayed quiet, watching Travis. Travis wasn't sure whether it was because he was being watched by Seth, or whether it was his commitment issues resurfacing, but he couldn't think of one thing to write. Everything that he started was swiftly scratched out. It was too corny, too cliché, too short; the list went on and on.

"Have you ever been out of the state?" Seth asked.

"No," Travis answered, annoyed.

"Well, maybe that's what's wrong with you then."

Travis faced him. "Excuse me?"

Seth pushed his plate out of the way. "You've never been out of Bumfuck, Egypt. So how do you know what you're missing?" Travis stared at him. "What I'm trying to say is for most guys about to get married, a kick-ass bachelor party cures them of their cold feet. Maybe what you need is a kick-ass road trip."

Travis turned and stared at the scribbled words on the paper. A road trip? There was no doubt in his mind that Rebecca would whole-heartedly agree with the outing. In a way, it was frustrating. Her selflessness was, for him, the most irritating thing about her. Never did she take what she wanted in consideration of whatever they were planning. But when it came to things that he wanted to do alone, it was, without a doubt, a relief.

"I've been across the entire fucking country before. I'll be the perfect guide," Seth continued.

"What? Were you in the army or something?" Travis eyed him suspiciously. He didn't look older than twenty—did he go AWL?

"The old man was. We traveled a lot when I was younger. I've done some of my own traveling," he added as an afterthought.

Travis stared dejectedly back at his scribbled notes. What was he thinking? He didn't know anything about the stranger next to him. This Seth guy could be fleeing from the law, a serial killer, or a terrorist. And yet... Travis shook his head to regain control of his thoughts. But the thought wouldn't—couldn't—escape: And yet, leaving Rebecca for a couple of days seemed like such a relief.

He gripped his pen tighter, nearly breaking it. Was he willing to risk losing Rebecca over a childish whim to see the country before committing himself? The shameful answer was yes, he was.

"Got a phone on you?" he asked Seth.

Seth smiled triumphantly and handed him his cell. Travis glared at the black phone before slowly punching in the numbers. Three rings. If she didn't answer by the fourth ring, he swore he was going to give up on this childish whim. She answered on the second ring.

"Hello?"

"Hey," he answered guiltily.

"Travis?"

"Yeah, I borrowed someone's phone."

"Is something wrong?" she asked. Panic saturated her voice.

"No, nothing's wrong. Actually, I wanted to ask you something..."

She waited patiently.

"I know this is sudden," he rushed, "but I was wondering if you would allow me to go on a little road trip?"

"We're getting married at the end of the week," she reminded him.

He bit his lip. Was she finally going to tell him no?

"Are you... afraid?" she finally asked.

How could she pick up on him so quickly, even without having to read his body language?

"A little," he admitted.

"Then you should go. If you think this will help, go ahead."

Her voice rang with sincerity. Wasn't she afraid that he'd leave her for good?

"But the wedding," he began. There had to be something he could say to assure her that he was going to return back to her.

"I'm sure you can get whatever it is out of your system in a week," she said. "But if you can't, or if you change your mind about *us*, well...You have my number."

"I *will* marry you," he swore. Why did she continuously allow herself to tell herself that he would leave her one day? "I promise you, we'll have a family and children."

"Stay safe, handsome," she said. He could hear the smile in her voice.

"I love you."

"And I you.'"

With a heavy sigh, he ended the call. Seth held out his hand, his fingers glittering with numerous rings. Travis returned the phone to its owner; it suddenly felt heavier, as if reflecting the large guilt that was forming in his heart, weighing him down.

"Head on home, get your things. I'll follow you and we'll leave in my car," Seth began.

"Why your car?" Travis frowned. He didn't like the sound of that. If he ended up missing, how were they going to find him?

Seth rolled his eyes. "Fine. Your car. I'll leave mine at your house, happy?"

"Don't you need to go home?"

He shook his head. "The things I need are in my car." He smiled. "I didn't want to go on a road trip by myself."

Travis took one last look at the scribbled notes. He laid down the money for his meal and a couple extra dollars for the waitress. Seth led the way out of the diner and Travis blindly followed him out into the afternoon sun, leaving behind the pad of paper and pen.

At first, he was uncomfortable with leaving Seth's car at his house. What would the neighbors say? But Seth had—by some sort of divine miracle—assuaged his fears. Who gave a fuck what the neighbors thought? The only person whose thoughts really mattered was his fiancée's, right? And didn't she give him the go ahead?

So Travis found himself reluctantly in the passenger seat of his own car. The backseat was crammed full of various suitcases. He, himself, only needed one. Travis didn't dare ask why Seth needed so many suitcases—he thought it would be wise to not know. The police would let him go when they knew he was totally oblivious; he was sure Seth was hiding something in there. Drugs, money, valuable artifacts, jewelry, maybe even chopped up pieces of someone. Who really knew?

Within a few hours, Travis found himself out of the state. Bumfuck, Egypt was completely behind him—and Rebecca. The radio station had been changed within a couple hours after they had set off, but the rock music was turned on low. Seth couldn't stand the music of the seventies, and Travis thought his ears would bleed with all the nonsense screaming that Seth appeared to comprehend. And thus, they compromised. The intense blaring and screaming would—and could—be tolerated at low volume.

Seth would stop every so often if there was a sight he thought Travis should see. By the time they had stopped for the night, Travis had been through three small towns, two parks, and seen numerous statues and monuments depicting ancient heroes and battles. But the greatest find was staring out the window, aimlessly watching the landscape change and unfold upon itself. To Travis' surprise, Seth turned out to be an excellent guide, though he didn't know exactly how much of the information Seth gave him was true. With every statue and monument that they stopped to see, Seth would ramble on about who it was and give a succinct biography, or he'd talk passionately about the battle that was fought and give a number of soldiers that had fought and the casualties.

For their meals, Seth refused to eat at the chain restaurants. The commercialized businesses, he proclaimed, were all communist bastards who needed a swift kick in the ass by good ol' Uncle Sam. But unfortunately, Uncle Sam's hands were in those bastards' pockets, so he was as corrupted as they were.

"But if the government is corrupted, then what's left?" Travis asked after taking a bite of steak. Seth had miraculously found a local restaurant amongst the glittering lights in a tourist town.

"'We the people', that's what's left. We need to stand up together and show those bastards who the boss is again. Do they fucking think they'd be in office right now if it weren't for us? Do those fucking communist bastards think they'd be rich without us? They treat us decently because if they didn't, we'd be after them. All three hundred and fifty fucking million of us."

Travis stared wide-eyed at him.

"Are you Christian?" Travis asked.

Seth stared at him like he'd gone insane. "Does it fucking matter?"

He looked sheepishly down at his food. "No, I guess it doesn't."

Everybody knows that you have to make a good first impression. They're vital to how other people perceive you as. And though Seth came off as an anarchist punk who didn't give a crap what people thought, Travis began looking at him differently. He was still a punk who didn't give a crap what people thought, but he definitely wasn't an anarchist—law and order needed to be maintained. He was smart, but rarely applied himself. He was energetic and passionate, but wanted to appear laid-back.

There were also the physical things Travis began to notice about his new friend. Though he frequently stomped, his movements were filled with grace. His chestnut eyes were framed by long lashes, and his face! Seth radiated with virility, and yet his face held such soft features and perfect skin. It was a face of an angel, putting all the women to shame, even Rebecca.

At times, Travis found himself completely mesmerized by Seth. Everything would be left forgotten except him. Travis watched his lips when he spoke, his hands when he said nothing. He often found himself shaking his eyes away and attempted to focus on the scenery, but his mind always replayed everything he had just observed of his friend.

And he could call Seth a friend now. They had been on the road for three days now, making it somewhere in the Midwest. He knew Seth's past, his old friends, and where he'd been. Likewise, Seth knew about the few ex-girlfriends Travis had, the future he saw with Rebecca, and where he had gone to college. The gap between them closed with every hour they were together; it frightened Travis and at the same time excited him.

"How's your wedding vows coming along?" Seth asked, placing Travis back to the real world.

The two of them had crashed for the night at a Holiday Inn somewhere off the highway. Though restaurant chains were communist bastards, hotel chains were fine. They needed to keep up a strict level of cleanliness, whereas local hotels and motels were a little sketchy. How many wary travelers disappeared from them and were never seen again? Travis had rolled his eyes at the statement; apparently Seth had watched a little too many horror movies.

"Not so good," Travis admitted, staring at the floor.

Seth had just stepped out of the shower, wearing nothing but a towel. His sable-hair was dripping wet. The water accentuated his toned body and left a trail down toward the towel that was wrapped carefully around his waist.

"Does my nakedness offend you?"

Travis felt a wave of heat rush to his cheeks. How long had it been since he last blushed? He looked up.

"No," he choked. Could anybody really look that perfect?

Seth smirked. "Good."

He grabbed his pack of cigarettes and lighter and stepped out onto the balcony. The cool night breeze that wafted through the room helped Travis' heart calm down. Why had it started to beat so wildly out of control? He stared out at the angel outside. Seth exhaled a plume of smoke and leaned onto the edge of the railing. Travis found himself staring at his friend once again. The moonlight cast a pale glow to Seth, illuminating him like a god.

Travis grabbed his toothbrush and toothpaste and headed quietly into the bathroom. The hot water of the shower helped calm him down. It made no sense to him. He had never been *attracted* to men before. It had always been women that he had chased and left broken. Why this one? Why now?

Cleaned and calm once again, Travis stepped out of the bathroom dressed only in sweats. Seth was no longer on the balcony. He was laying casually on his bed in boxers, watching television. He acknowledged Travis and turned his attention back toward the screen. Some mindless reality show was on. Travis felt a blush creep into his cheeks and was suddenly grateful the lights were out. Seth hadn't gawked at him when he came out of the shower. Seth had never stared at him, mesmerized by his very movements.

Travis crept into bed and lay on his side—away from Seth. There was something seriously wrong with him. Maybe, Travis thought to himself, it was Seth's angelic face. It was something to behold. And it had been awhile since he had seen Rebecca. Since they'd been together, they had only been away from each other for a few hours due to work.

"Nervous about going back?" Seth asked.

"Yeah," he lied.

"Don't worry about it. You'll find the right words to say when the day arrives, even if you didn't write it down on a fucking piece of paper."

"Thanks," he said.

Travis slowly drifted to sleep and dreamed of Seth.

Seth began the drive back. He kept assuring Travis that he was going to get him back in time for his wedding—even if that meant driving the car down the aisle. Travis had smiled, but said nothing. He didn't notice anything outside, unless Seth pointed something out. The music had been turned back to music of the seventies, but much to Travis' surprise, he found he liked the nonsense screaming and blaring of rock that Seth preferred much better. He turned it back; Seth glanced at him but said nothing.

Since dreaming of Seth, his friend had suddenly filled his

mind. He couldn't—or rather wouldn't—shake him away from his thoughts. And though he tried to stop it, he couldn't even slow down the ever closing gap the two had had in the beginning. It felt to Travis that the two of them had grown up together or at least known each other much longer than a few days. And even though he was going to get married—the commitment suddenly seemed even more frightening the closer they got back home—Travis knew he wanted to continue to stay friends with Seth long after he dropped Travis back home. But Travis also knew that staying friends with him was only an excuse to be with him and stare at him. Seth had become his obsession and his darkest desire. Was it wrong of him?

"Looks like you'll make it to your wedding after all," Seth said as soon as they had settled into their recent hotel room.

Travis nodded his head absently.

"Something wrong? You look like shit."

Travis stiffened. His obsession was suddenly in front of him, his chestnut orbs studying him speculatively. His breath smelled of cigarettes. Travis took in a deep breath and attempted to remain calm.

"No, nothing's wrong."

Seth studied him a moment longer and then turned to smoke outside. Travis let out his breath slowly. He had been so close . . . too close. If Seth had leaned in a little closer, Travis was afraid he may have acted upon his dreams and kissed him.

"I should have you back within four hours tomorrow," Seth said from the balcony. He took a long drag from his cigarette and exhaled slowly. "What time did you say your wedding was?"

Travis leaned against the sliding glass doors. "Six." He looked away.

Seth smirked. "Will your fiancée be pissed that you missed the rehearsal dinner?"

"No," he said quickly.

"What about if you miss your wedding?"

"Not if it was what I wanted," he admitted.

Seth took one last puff and dropped the cigarette to the ground, extinguishing it with his shoe. He walked determinedly toward Travis with a look in his eye that Travis couldn't identify. He suddenly looked *dangerous*. Travis backed away into the room, but Seth kept following him until he felt a wall behind him. Seth had him trapped. Did everyone's murderer look so beautiful, or was he the only lucky one?

"Tell me something," Seth whispered, placing his hands on either side of Travis' head.

Travis allowed himself to look into Seth's eyes. All the fight he had been building up melted away.

"What?" he breathed.

"Why the fuck have I been catching you staring at me during our little fucking journey?"

"Because I want you," he answered, afraid to lie. He mentally kicked himself. If Seth was going to spare him before, he surely wasn't anymore.

Seth leaned in and whispered in his ear, "Want to know a secret? I've wanted you since I saw you at the diner. I thought it would be interesting to see if I could convert a straight man my way. I was planning for a challenging fuck and then I'd fucking leave you like trash."

Travis trembled. Seth's hot breath sent his heart into erratic palpitations.

"But I wasn't expecting my trash to be my own treasure," Seth whispered.

Travis sucked in a deep breath and suddenly found Seth's lips crashing down on his. All the resistance he had been building and carefully maintaining came crashing down upon contact. There was no way he could deny the feelings he felt toward Seth any longer. He loved him and his life gravitated around this man. Rebecca would be crushed—that was certain—but would she deny him of being with the one that so completed him? He did still love Rebecca, but her hands didn't send flames trailing down his arms, nor was she so perfect, so *beautiful*. Seth was his god and Travis didn't care what rule he broke to be exiled from Olympus.

By the time the dawn broke, revealing the two locked in each other's embrace, Travis knew that between Rebecca and Seth, he couldn't live without Seth.

"So what's the verdict on Rebecca?" Seth asked, tuning Travis back to reality.

Travis turned toward his lover and friend. "I think you're right. I owe her big time," he agreed.

Seth nodded in agreement. "You stayed with me on the day you were supposed to be married, without even giving her a call. I still can't fucking believe the words that came flying out of her mouth when you told her about us."

Travis laughed. "It's so unlike her."

"But she couldn't help it. I'd do the same if my world was taken from me."

Travis looked up to see Seth standing before him. His hair was brushed neatly and he was smartly dressed in a suit. Though he still wore his many piercings, he had left them out—for now anyway. Travis couldn't look away. Seth brushed the back of his palm across Travis' cheek.

"You're my world, my treasure," Seth muttered before placing a kiss on his lips. "And I know you love her still, but not as strongly as you love me. You promised her a family with children. Give them to her. And maybe, just maybe ... she'll return the favor and give us children of our own."

Travis leaned back and looked into his deep chestnut orbs. "Seth?"

He smirked and kissed him lightly.

"Someday, I'd like us to raise a child of our own."

"You're not exactly the perfect father figure." Travis frowned.

"And you're not exactly the perfect mother figure." Seth smiled and neatly dodged the pillow that was thrust in his direction.

His laughter filled the apartment until he left. Travis sighed and watched the growing crowds outside. It wasn't complete yet, but he thought he could see it. The carving the designer had so meticulously shaped out of bare rock was about to be finished. The intricate details that littered the carving were finished. The designer just had to shape out the rough edges. A house, a family, and a dog. Things he thought he would never have once he chose his life with Seth. Things he had promised to the woman he thought he couldn't live without. These simple things would—and could—be granted.

If you thought "Summer" was a bubble gum story, think again. This oozes sweetness and all things that are cute about falling in love with your best friend. I was inspired to write this after viewing a picture of a girl puckering up with a frog in her hand. It was a well done photoshoot and I couldn't help but take another stab at a fairy tale, this time *The Frog Prince.*

L'Amour

Every little girl has been told that her Prince Charming will sweep her off her feet and they'll live happily ever after. And then you grow up and find out those fairy tales were nothing but myths, fabrications. Prince Charming doesn't exist and perfect happiness died out long ago.

***

Rain poured, washing away all of the pain and memories associated with what was us. It was a much needed cleansing. Love had blinded me, so I was told. He wasn't the perfect man I had thought he was and he left me for the next pretty face that looked his way. The pain resonated through me; no amount of cold could numb it out.

I wasn't too sure how long I had been standing there after he had told me it was over and left. He just walked away from me, without looking back. It struck me like an arrow to the heart. My heart clenched, waking me from my daze momentarily. There was one thought that resonated through my mind during that split second when I became aware of my surroundings: Run. So I ran. I wasn't sure where I was headed—I just needed to leave to find my Wonderland. My legs seemed to know where the white rabbit had disappeared to. Branches and foliage dared to scratch me when I burst through into a forest.

The rain wasn't as heavy here thanks to the thick canopy. A calm silence permeated the area. Had I actually stepped through the looking-glass? My eyes took in the small stream nearby as I caught my breath.

"What are you doing here?"

I turned, expecting the Mad Hatter or Cheshire Cat. Instead I found Eric, my best friend. I hadn't seen much of him since I had been going out with my now ex-boyfriend.

"I...don't know," I finally answered.

He glanced around. "No boyfriend?"

"We...broke up." I shrugged, telling myself that this happens all the time. "What are you doing here?" I finally asked.

"It's a place I go to if I want to think. I showed it to you once, remember?"

I nodded, allowing the memory to permeate my mind. A *ribbit* distracted me; I crouched down low and moved closer to the stream. I found the little frog nestled between a couple of rocks. He was such a small frail thing. He started to move away, but I managed to capture him in time.

Eric walked near me. "What are you going to do with the little guy?"

I straightened. "Remember the fairy tale, 'The Frog Prince'? Maybe if I kiss him, he'll turn into a prince and all of this *pain* will just go away."

I cupped the frog more carefully in my hands and closed my eyes. Sure it was weird and a bit gross to be kissing frogs, but I needed *something* to make my heart stop hurting. And hope—even if I knew it wouldn't work—was there to alleviate the pain, even if a little. I placed a light kiss on the frog's head and opened my eyes.

I gave an empty smile. "Guess it didn't work."

Eric grabbed my wrist, forcing me to look at him. "Or maybe it did." He leaned down, glancing at me hesitantly before placing a gentle kiss on my lips.

"Maybe it did," I whispered back.

This is my favorite story. I can't even recall how I came up with the idea. But I wrote this story and then found out about Writer's Digest short story competition. Unfortunately, I didn't win or even make it in the finals, but I'm really satisfied with how it turned out.

Confession

"Forgive me Father, for I have sinned," a man said. His voice was angelic.

I nodded as I sat in the dark confession booth. It had been a long day and this was the last of the confessions. "When was your last confession?" I asked as I straightened my robes.

The man hesitated, "I don't remember."

I glanced at the screen. "You shouldn't lie during a confession."

"It's been a long time, Father... I'm... I'm too embarrassed to say, and even I can't tell you how long it has been. I just know it's been many, many years."

Sighing, I waved my hand. "Proceed."

I heard the man shift in his seat. "I have a very long confession..."

"And I'll be sure to hear all of it, my child. No matter how long it takes."

The man sighed again and thus, began his tale...

———————◆———————

"Please, Father, refrain from interrupting me for, like I said, my tale is long. I was a man that was beheld by all. I had reached the top and was favored by all, but I wanted more. I wanted to be served, I didn't want to serve. Thus, I was shut out. There have been many things that I have done since then, but I confessed to all during my last confession, and feel no need to bring it up here.

"I come here today to confess of the crimes I have partaken in. Things that my servants have done that, I regret to say, I have enjoyed because it's an act of revenge against the man who has shut me out.

"There are many, many things that I have done and alas, I do not remember all. But I will start with the most recent of things that I have done...One that I can certainly say was my doing, because of greed, is the oil spill in the Gulf. This world that He has created is so vast and rich, but I'm afraid that I've become envious of his doing. I have seeped the minds of many; it wasn't hard to do, and because of me, hundreds of animals that He loved are gone and the ocean is now tainted with black. I admit, Father, that I take some pleasure in knowing that His work isn't so perfect anymore.

"I have been with many that have gone to war and I have been the one to tell each leader that they are the right ones. From the War on Terror, to World War I, the American Civil War, and even as early back to the Crusades and even earlier still, I have always been there whispering glories in their ears. Millions have died for what they thought was right, and He has felt every death stinging in his side.

"Some of the things that I have been most proud of are my abilities to conjure up plagues and famines, as He is able to do so, and I wish to be like Him. The Black Plague was brilliant. His children wondered what they had done wrong to deserve such a cruel death, and nobody suspected that it was me. Even the Great Famine during the Depression, they thought it was He who called upon the locusts, but it was rather I.

"I have been among His children, whispering of greatness that they could claim if they followed at my side. Some of my followers have become legends: Jack the Ripper and Charles Manson.

"Thus I come today to confess of these crimes that I have partaken in."

"I am sorry for these and all the sins of my life," the man concluded.

I glanced at the screen. "Are you telling me the truth?"

"Aren't I supposed to tell the truth during these things?"

A shiver ran down my spine as he turned to glance toward the screen. It felt as if he was looking through me, into my very soul. Something about this man was strange...

"What's your name?"

"I thought these were supposed to be anonymous...?"

His voice was still angelic, but I suddenly noticed, there was a slight roughness to it. It was raw and primeval, almost—dare I say it?—demonic.

"Er, yes, that's right." I sat back and thought about what the man had said. If everything he said really was true...I glanced back at the screen. The man was staring back at me, waiting for me to finish.

"These crimes are grave indeed," I began, "If what you say is true then I'm not sure where you can even begin to atone for these crimes. Perhaps you should try to gain the forgiveness of this man whom shut you out."

"That's why I am here, Father. This is the one place that He will always listen."

"Will you ever stop?"

I thought a saw a glimmer of a smile through the screen. "Maybe..."

"Maybe?"

"I want to reach the top no matter what it takes."

I narrowed my eyes. "Then there is nothing I can do for you."

"Should I say the Act of Contrition?"

"You won't stop. So why should I or God forgive you?"

The man sighed and stood up, making his way out of the booth. I heard him stop outside just beyond the curtain that barricaded me from the church.

"Perhaps in another thousand years I'll try to be forgiven, but it's difficult because your kind has never quite forgiven me for being the cause of your abandonment from Paradise. But here's a question for you: If you, who are so Holy and in His service has been a faithful servant, why hasn't He forgiven you and allowed you into Paradise? That man isn't as forgiving as you might think." He made his way out of the booth.

I pushed the curtain roughly aside. "Who are you to talk of the

Lord like that?" I demanded. But nobody was there. On the floor, right where the man should have been was a shiny, red apple and balancing precariously on top was an olive branch.

Not a short story or flash fiction, but this is the only poem I've ever written that I'm proud to admit that I wrote. (I will never be a poet.) My great-grandmother had just passed away and I felt compelled to compose something in her honor. This poem is the result.

Guardian

I wish that I could've known you a lot more than I did,
To listen to your stories about your childhood,
And watch that dreamy look come upon your face.
I was the unlucky grandchild I suppose, not being able to know you
for all my life like the others,
But you were always so nice to me, treating me as part of the family.
I'll remember that, and remember everything you said,
Your great image still lingering in my head, never to go.
I always seemed to live in a fantasy,
Always thinking that you'd live forever, never thinking once that
you'd have to go someday.
But now I know, that was just a selfish thought.
I came back to reality, and it hurts so much.
You lived through so much, what exciting stories they must have
been, like how you felt
during World War II and JFK's assassination.
But now you're a guardian angel watching over us,
Protecting each and every one of us from harm.

Nos sunt velle revocare tu semper.
(We are willing to remember you always)

This was written just a couple months after I turned 20.

There was a contest on DeviantArt where writers were told to create a story based off this statue. It was a really compelling statue with a pretty girl, Flame, who looked severely burnt and had bandages wrapped around her. And then there was this little figure latched on her that looked like a pile of ash but it had a face.

I had some initial problems coming up with a story for her, but I knew that I wanted to write her story. Whether I made it on time for the contest deadline, it mattered not.

I believe it was a day before the deadline or the day of the deadline that I sat down and watched the "It Gets Better" short film that Pixar released on YouTube. And I realized that the girl was a victim of bullying. I suddenly had a story! I wrote it as fast as I could and did some minor editing and sent it in. To my surprise, I managed to get an honorable mention.

Flame and Ash

In my very first memory, there's an intense heat. I can hear wood crackling; I can feel my skin blistering. And there's a deep, grumbling voice somewhere nearby..."You really did it this time..."

My memory replays itself night after night in my dreams. My eyes open at the same time my dream self does, but instead of flames I see a white ceiling and the sound of monitors and gadgets beeping tickle my eardrums.

"Remember anything?" my nurse asks as she walks in to check my vitals. She asks me every morning. And every morning, I would answer,

"No. Nothing."

She flashes me a sympathetic smile and changes the bandages on my face. Her hands graze my scars—I had at first protested, but grew to endure it; it made me feel like I was something other than just a part of the room that I had grown to become a part of. Before she leaves for the morning, my nurse provides me with a bland breakfast that I would eventually eat. The television was always blaring some mindless show and I would stare out the window and wonder what it was like to be a free bird.

My existence was based upon an endless routine, which for Jane Does like me should stay uninterrupted. But maybe all routines were meant to be broken...Or at least that's what I thought until my nurse returned earlier than expected, dropping a package on my lap.

"What is it?"

"A package of course," she answers as she writes feverishly in my chart. "It was addressed to 'Our Most Forgetful Jane Doe'."

I trace my hands over the package. "What's in it?"

"Dunno. Open it and see!" She plops down next to me. Her excitement is contagious—my hands begin to quiver as I open it.

A large, heavy book with a ton of ash was the only thing in the package. I brush the ash off and open the cover. In a neat handwriting, the words 'Property of Flame' was written at the top.

"Mean anything to you?"

I flip through the pages. They are filled with bizarre text and none of which make any sense to me. I shake my head.

"Aww. Well maybe it will. Let me clean up the pile of... ash?..." She looks at my blankets which are now strangely ash free. "Strange...Well I'll see you later."

I dreamt of a time much older than ours. People were protesting my existence outside of a castle. The king valiantly attempted to appease the rioting crowd as I was led away to a secret chamber.

The bodiless voice that continuously haunted my dreams muttered, "Ignorant people. We're trying to help them, not destroy them." His voice was saturated with a Scottish accent—something I've never noticed before.

I opened my mouth to reply, but the voice began speaking again: quicker and more urgent than before.

"Come on lass. Wake up! Wake up!"

My eyes open and I find myself staring straight into the piercing yellow eyes of a pile of ash. Its eyes illuminate the dark room; a wispy stream of smoke emit from it.

"Flame! I finally found you!"

I jump. Piles of ash are not supposed to speak. Ever.

"Don't you remember me?" The ash moves closer to my face. It has the same deep, grumbling, Scottish accent as the bodiless voice in my dreams.

"Um, no. Don't remember a pile of talking ash in my life." I take a deep breath. "I must be dreaming. My subconscious mind is trying to file my memories of the fire and the hospital into one thing."

"This isn't a dream lass. I've come to take you back."

I laugh. It sounds forced. Perhaps it is or maybe I really don't know how to laugh. "Back? Back where?"

"Home of course."

"And where exactly is home?"

The little pile of ash shifts his gaze to my new reading material. "Home is the book?"

"Don't be silly lass! How could anyone live in a book?" He glares at me.

"Who are you anyway?"

He huffs himself up. "Ash of course. I'm your tutor, well, more like your master of sorts." Ash shifts himself to more comfortable position. "I taught you in the arts of magic."

"Magic?" I raise an eyebrow. What was in that soup my nurse served me for supper?

He closes his eyes in serious thought. "Yes. Magic. Your element was fire, of course. It's how you got your name." His piercing eyes open again and settle upon me, blazing into my soul. "That book can get you back home—to your right time lass."

"My right time? What exactly do you mean?" I sit up all the way, staring at the strange little pile of talking ash.

He turns and looks out the window. "This isn't where you belong lass." His gaze shifts toward me. "We're from a much older time..."

Sharp pangs ring through my skull. People crying out freak, demon, monster... I was a monster... A she-devil who shouldn't exist. Memories flitter at the edges of my consciousness.

"No...No..." I grab my head and shake it, hoping that the memories will cease. "I don't belong there!"

"Now Flame, don't say that. It's your proper time. Of course you belong there. Now that little accident you caused before you disappeared on us, don't worry about it. Got it all taken care of."

I raise the blankets over me. "They don't like me. The people think I'm a demon." I still don't remember the accident, but I refuse to let Ash know.

The wisp of smoke that streams from Ash's body moves the blankets away, so he can see me better. "Sure you may look different and sure you know some magic lass, but chin up. It gets better."

I shrug the smoke away. "I like it here better." The people don't call me a freak. The people here always smile at me. They always try to make me happy. But the people from my memories—the memories that I just remembered—they don't like me and I fear that further memories will only confirm that fact. I doubt anyone from my actual time liked me at all. With the exception of Ash. He seems to like me. At least, I think so.

Ash hops on top of my book. "Fine. Stay here for all I care. You're caged in here, you know until they see fit that you're all better. Though they'll want you to pay them money for taking care of you. I'm sure you owe a fine little fortune as of now."

"The nurse, she likes me. She's nice to me," I mutter lamely.

Ash rolls his eyes. "Of course she's nice to you. She's nice to all her patients."

"They don't call me a monster."

Ash heaves the book open and begins flipping through the pages. "Of course they haven't, lass. You've been in a hospital. They take care of people. They've seen people look worse than you. Walk out of here and people will either feel sympathetic or stay away from you because you look the way you do." He turns, the smoke continuing to flip through the pages. "Don't you want to return back and help people? That's what you were training for: helping people. You wanted people to see past your face. You wanted to prove that magic wasn't just for conjuring up destruction."

I look away and watch as it begins to rain softly outside.

"I can do all of that here," I whisper.

"In this time you'll only be seen as a form of entertainment. Not a healer. No one will take you seriously."

I continue to watch the rain fall. It's interesting how rain washes everything away. Water is a wonderful element—the life-giver. I sigh. I wish that was my element. Instead I was stuck with the destructive force of fire.

"Look Flame. You were lucky. You were reborn into this time. Now it's time to grow up again and face your fears. What do you say?"

He had finally stopped turning pages. I grab the book and take a look at the pages. They are filled with strange pictures with triangles and circles and the text was still unreadable to me. I hadn't unlocked my memories of magic. All I remember is the unending cycle of pain.

"I don't remember what this says."

Ash gives me a wide smile. "That's all right. We'll just have to start from scratch." He hops over and nestles himself on the side of my face. I can feel the heat of his body permeating through my bandages that cover the hideous scar that marks me as a monster. "I promise you lass, it will get better." He pats me on the head and the teaching begins again.

I found this flash fiction buried in a folder. It's actually something that I've written rather recently (within the past year, I think). It's a bit rusty since I haven't written anything short in quite some time due to being focused on my novels, but I still find it kind of enjoyable.

Inspired by a prompt from Mistress of the Dark Path's monthly writing challenge.

Snowballed

Billy peeked around the large mountain of snow; he could see his breath. The older boys were hiding somewhere within the forest—the only line of color as far as the eye could see. He hunkered down and rubbed his hands together, hoping to regain some circulation. His mittens lay forgotten on the ice adjacent to him—the snow stuck to them, making it hard to roll a perfect snowball.

He took another peek at the forest lining. A shadow moved. Was it the enemy? A lump of terror rose to his throat. No. He had to stay strong! He had to do this! He had... Billy froze as another shadow moved. Two. There were two that he could clearly spot. Where were the other three?

He hunkered back down behind the hill, hoping no one had spotted him. Unless the older boys noticed his shock of red hair beneath his white toboggan, Billy assumed he'd be hard to spot in the snowy landscape with his pale skin and white coat. It made sense to him to ask for a white winter ensemble. With the blinding white snow, perfectly untouched in this field, it was the perfect camouflage. This year he would beat the older boys and prove he wasn't some child.

A crunch alerted him. Billy stole a peek around his hill. He didn't see anyone... but someone caused the snow to crunch. He scooped up some snow and began packing it into a tight ball. His hands were red from being exposed in the elements for so long.

Crunch!

Billy's heart raced. His grip tightened around the snowball.

Crunch!

Did the older boys know where he was? Was all his planning for naught?

Crunch! Crunch! Crunch!

"I swear he was around here," a voice said from afar.

"Probably fled like the little wuss he is."

Billy dropped his current snowball and rolled up more. He needed ammunition. The enemy was so close...

"I knew he'd run. Any kid who's got any sense would run," Billy heard the boy spit.

For a moment, Billy stopped. It *was* crazy to go up against five experienced older boys. Maybe the best thing to do was to run...

No. He shook his head. The leader of the pack, Johnny, had crossed the line. If he and his friends had just bullied Billy, Billy would've been fine with that. He would've never felt the need to do something as stupid as this. But Johnny—no, that *jerk*—had insulted his family. Called his sister a—dare he say it?—slut for being pregnant out of wedlock! Said his father was a poor drunken slob that wasn't any war hero, but a coward, and his mother was a dirty whore.

Fueled by the memory of the insults, Billy became enraged and gripped the snowball until his knuckles turned white. He stood up, took aim, and flung it straight at Johnny's head. The pack of boys immediately huddled around their leader, protecting him from the onslaught of snowballs. Billy had blood pounding in his ears, deafening him, so he didn't hear the first pleas to stop until he saw one of the boys crying. Billy dropped his snowball. He had made one of them cry! A swell of victory swooped through him until he realized Johnny was bleeding; he had been cut by a rock that had accidentally slipped its way inside the snowball.

Johnny's right hand man stood up as Billy neared to get a better look at Johnny's swollen face. And the blood! His nose was like a faucet of blood.

"I should kick your ass for what you did to Johnny!" the second in command threatened.

Billy didn't flinch or cower. His eyes were glued onto Johnny's face. *He* had done that?

"No," Johnny said in a hoarse whisper. "He's proved that he's no kid anymore. Let 'im go."

The boy glanced at Johnny reluctantly, but did as he said. The other boys followed suit and shifted out of Billy's way as he strode passed them, never looking back.

The more I look over this short story, the more I see the many problems with it. Staying in short story form is restricting it, especially in terms of characterization and plot. There are many unanswered questions, which is why I plan on expanding this story into a novel.

This was inspired by a very vivid dream I had. For once, I was the main character of my own dream and it was interesting to see things in first person POV. I'm usually more of an observer in my dreams.

I mulled it over for a couple of months on whether or not I should write it down and then while on vacation, decided "Why not?" So I began work on it on vacation sometime during the summer of 2006 and didn't get it finished until about October.

Mine

America. The great melting pot. Ironically enough, most people won't accept you if you're not white. For people like me, who aren't, who exactly am I? They say to embrace who you are if you want to "fit in". Well, I don't know what to embrace.

"Susan, you should smile more," my mother told me flatly as she drove the van down the country lane.

I was staring out the window. Blurs of what I thought was corn and soy swept by. She always told me to smile more, but what for? I sighed when she made the comment, showing that although I didn't want to hear it, I was listening. My eyes quickly darted toward her. She was what most people called an Asian beauty. Soft features with perfectly shaped almond eyes that held the mysteries of the world. Then there was me: the Asian that had a nose too big for my face. It deteriorated my soft features, features that I inherited from my mother. The nose came from nowhere. But my pride and joy was my hair, and people loved it.

I saw her frown from my response, if you can call a sigh a response, and without any second thoughts about it, my eyes darted back to the country scenery.

Fields upon fields of never ending farmland continued to sweep by. On occasion I saw a horse, or a herd of cows, but mostly, in this small area of nowhere, it was mainly crops.

"You're not going to show your grandmothers that same attitude, are you?" I heard her ask with authority.

"What do you think?" I threw back at her. The car stopped abruptly and I was pulled forward by the force. My eyes grew wide, as I looked wildly at her. Just as I was about to yell at her, she glared at me from her seat, towering over me, though I was a couple inches taller.

"Susan, I mean it. I'm sick of your I-don't-care-about-the-world attitude! You need to shape up," she said icily.

"So why'd you insist on taking me anyway?" My voice was raised slightly, but I was too frightened to yell at her. I may have never respected her like I should have, but I did have enough sense to know my limits.

My body was soon propelled back as she turned to continue to drive down the lane. She was silent for a moment, as if she was collecting her thoughts. As I started to forget my question, my mother answered back, just above a whisper, "Tangshinun kairichidarul p'iryo haeyo."

I looked quizzically at her. I hated it when she answered my questions in Korean. There was one point in life when I thought it was neat, but the aggravation of learning a new language didn't bode well on me, so I stopped. I guess, I never really tried. The only word I understood was a simple 'hello' and beyond that, nothing.

I grew to hate my mother's light accent. I hated my ancestors. I hated my heritage. I hated my customs. But what I hated the most was being labeled different. I didn't want to be different, I wanted to be normal. I wanted to be the blonde-haired, blue-eyed cheerleader who dated the quarterback of the football team. I wanted to be that prom queen. I wanted to be that girl with admirers who swooned every time she smiled at them. I would have even settled on being the goth girl because even she was considered more normal than I.

Within a few minutes of guessing what my mother had told me, the scenery slowly changed. Quaint buildings could be seen here and there fighting against the farmland. Slowly, slowly, more and more buildings popped up until we entered the edge of a small town. Grandma's street was the main road, and it wasn't too hard to find her house either.

My mother turned onto a long driveway with a modern brick home with a touch of Oriental flair. The roof was the most obvious of all the Oriental touches put on the home. I groaned when I saw it, it was just another thing to hate.

"Annyong haseyo!" my grandma called out as we got out of the van. She was a short woman, with wrinkles showing under her eyes. Her head was a bit square-ish, and her hair was short, grey, and curled. She came running down, which looked more like a waddle to me, to embrace my mother.

"Annyong haseyo!" my mother replied cheerfully, returning the hug to her mother-in-law.

"Yeah, hi," I muttered with a curt wave.

My grandma looked up at me with a frown. Her perfectly shaped almond eyes surveyed me. "Ah, Susan! You're looking as lovely as ever, but do you have to wear such big shirts?" She placed her hands on my large, dark blue hoodie, trying to find where the fabric stopped and my body began. Finding my stomach, she frowned again. "Look at this! You're so skinny! People will think you're fat if you continue to wear these big clothes! You should be proud and show off your fine figure!"

"There's nothing pretty about me," I sighed.

I noticed my mother's look when I said that. It was almost the exact same look she had given me when I threw that question back at her in the car. I swiftly diverted my eyes away from her and gave the best fake smile I could offer at my grandma. She accepted it and began throwing hundreds of questions at my mother. I was afraid she wouldn't be able to answer them all at such a fast rate, but she somehow did. The conversation started out in English for the sake of me, but in the short time it took to walk from the van to the door of the house, it had deteriorated into Korean.

Just as I was about to step into the house, Grandma stopped me. "Your great-grandmother wants you. Why don't you visit her?"

Remembering my mother's stern look, I decided to humor Grandma. It was the least I could do, and besides, it was better than sitting in the house, listening to Korean, while flipping aimlessly at the television to find there was nothing on at all in over 300 channels.

Sighing, I finally asked with a light smile, "Where is she?"

"In the shop of course." She indicated the small white building in the back that I had at first mistaken for a garage. As I began to walk up the long winding driveway, I heard her announce with an air of mischievousness, "If you can find her."

I turned in confusion at my grandma, but she had already walked into the house. I honestly didn't want to meet my great-grandma because of the language barrier. She was born and raised in Korea, thereby only knowing Korean. It was Grandpa that insisted she come and live with them when he moved to America. It frustrated me trying to talk to her, but she just smiled at me, as if the language barrier never bothered her once. I dragged myself to the shop, forcing myself to move my feet with each step I took. The shop came closer and closer, and before I knew it, I had reached the little white shop.

The bells clanged against one another lightly as I opened the door. The shop smelled of must, and if it weren't for the screen door bringing in some light, I wouldn't have been able to see anything.

"Hello?" I called out uncertainly. Silence answered. Frowning, I timidly took a few steps into the shop, squinting here and there to see if I could make anything out. "Where's the light switch?" I found myself thinking out loud.

As I said that, a dull light dilatorily illuminated from beneath me, starting a chain of lights scattered throughout. I gasped suddenly at the sight before me, taking in a quick intake of dust. I bent over, coughing roughly, but I wanted to make sure I saw everything right. There, just beyond where I was standing was a couple of wooden planks leading to a rock column. The column had more wooden planks that led to another column, and the pattern continued far out of view. There was another path to my right that looked as if it went down, and another to my left that went across. All around me was complete darkness and cold air. I had a sense of being in an underground cavern somewhere, and nearly screamed when I found out I was standing on a cliff. I couldn't see the bottom and the drop was steep. There were no ledges for me to grab on if I fell, and nobody but Grandma knew I was out here. What kind of a shop had a cavern as you walked in? I tried to peer down into the abyss, balancing myself carefully so I wouldn't fall. As I looked over the edge, a gust of cold air shot up, blowing into my face, and blowing my hair straight up.

I stood up and looked back to the door, only to find the door was no more. Frantically looking around, I found that there was nowhere else to go but on one of the paths. I wanted to go forward, and the only one that *looked* like it went forward was the path in front of me, the path that led up.

Heaving myself to go on, I decided to take a short breather at the column I was standing on. I watched as the last column's light I was on, faded out. The one ahead slowly faded on. I breathed heavily and plopped down with a hand over my heart. My eyes drifted back to the blackness, and I found myself doubting my choice. Had I gone the right way? I had been walking aimlessly on the path of wooden planks and rock columns for the past fifteen minutes and I was getting nowhere fast. But then, just as I was thinking about walking back down, in the hopes that the door I had walked in would somehow appear out of nowhere, a bird chirped.

The chirping came from above me, and when I looked up I saw a pretty white bird. It was decorated with a tinge of pale yellow on its crest and pale red cheeks. My first guess was a cockatiel, but the bird was larger than most cockatiels I've ever seen in the pet shops. Still, the bird seemed to have cast a spell on me, and I soon found myself following it the rest of the way up the path.

It chirped, circled around me, and swept through the gateway I found myself standing in front of. It was tall, wooden, with red rectangles and squares swooping off and flapping on its sides. There was black lettering on the small flags, and when I squinted at it, I realized the message, whatever it said, was written in Hangul, the

Korean alphabet. I hesitated at the gateway. Because the gateway reminded me of the archway of a shrine, I was unsure to enter. It held a forbidden feel to it. I couldn't even really see beyond it and looked back again to the path I had just stepped off of. But the bird chirped insistently this time from the other side, and I found myself taking my first few steps beyond the gateway.

What I found wasn't exactly what I wanted to find. Stacks and stacks of boxes surrounded me. The cardboard boxes were larger than me, and to my luck, "More wooden planks." I smirked in disbelief.

This time the planks led in all sorts of directions, so I was unsure of where exactly to go. But the bird swooped into my line of eyesight and out, only to reappear flying along one of the paths. Before I knew it, I was following it. Where it was leading me, I didn't know, nor did I care. This bird captivated me, piqued my curiosity. I had to know where it was going, why it was trapped in a shop that appeared to be minute.

I found myself running along the edge of a rather large tower of cardboard boxes, attempting to keep up with the bird, when a blinding white light hit my eyes. Instinctively, I put my hands up to guard my eyes, but when I looked again, I saw a doorway leading outside. Blue skies and marshmallow clouds met me when I walked out. Tentatively, I looked over the railing.

The small town where my grandmothers lived spread out before me, the wind playing lightly with my hair. I moved a few stubborn strands out of my face, and gasped. This small town, a town I thought held such little value, looked so beautiful from where I was.

I was higher than I thought I was, up on the edge of a concrete building. Had I really traveled this long distance? A chirp diverted my attention to my right, where I noticed a fleet of stairs. Looking back down to the town, I took a deep breath and began the ascent.

———————◆———————

It was only a mere three flights, something I walked up and down nearly every day at school. And yet, by the time I reached the top I was out of breath and found myself staring at a door. Unsure, I placed my hand on the handle of the door. After what seemed like hours, I drew the courage to open it.

A wind chime sounded when I opened the door, and a whaf of spiced, sour, pickled, cabbage hit my nose. There was no mistake about that smell, it was the smell of Korea's staple food besides rice: kimchi. I found myself inside a small, Oriental store. Garlic hung from the ceiling in strings, looking like thick icicles. Their smell mixed lightly with the kimchi, making it somewhat tolerable to look around.

"Annyong haseyo," an elderly voice said from my left.

Jumping from surprise, I looked to find my great-grandma. She was dressed in a simple white hanbok, the traditional dress of Korea. Grandma always looked old and tired, but Great-Grandmother was just the opposite. Despite her old age, she didn't look a day older than fifty. Not one wrinkle decorated her face, and her long, silky, black hair was kept in a neat braid.

I smiled delicately at her. "Um...*annyong haseyo?*"

Great-Grandmother gave me a wide smile. "Ne, ne. Idiwa," she told me gently, patting the counter before her.

My brow furrowed at her statement, unsure of what she was saying, but I interpreted that she wanted me to come to her. I crossed the short distance between us, and before I knew it, I hurled a rough question at her. "Where are we?"

She continued to smile at me, not even giving a response in Korean. It killed me. The peace I had found while making my way to her was slowly deteriorating. I just couldn't take it anymore, and I began shouting, screaming, yelling at this poor old woman who didn't know what I was saying. All she knew was that I was upset.

"WHERE ARE WE? WHAT ARE YOU DOING UP HERE? WHAT DID YOU WANT? I'M SICK OF YOU! I DON'T WANT TO SEE YOU AGAIN! JUST TELL ME WHAT YOU WANT!"

Her smiling expression turned worrisome in a matter of a few seconds. It hurt me, I won't lie. This kind old woman, my great-grandmother, was being yelled at by some brat and she didn't even deserve it. I guess I was more frustrated than I thought. It was then that she pulled out a ticket and handed it to me. She pointed her finger at me and said with finality, "Tangshinun. Susan. Tangshinun."

"For…me?" I asked, pointing at myself.

She nodded. "Susan."

I took the ticket, a train ticket, and walked slowly out, ready to make the long journey back down. But to my surprise, I was outside of the quaint white building, on solid ground. Grandma's house was within my eyesight. I opened the door again, the wind chimes indicating the door opening. There she was, my great-grandma, looking peacefully at me. I waved good-bye slowly before heading back down the winding driveway.

"Hello Susan," Grandma said calmly as I walked in.

I looked at her curiously. Did she know about Great-Grandmother? "Where's the train station?"

"The train station?" My grandma and mom exchanged looks. A small smile appeared on my mom's face. "You'll find it at the opposite end of the town," Grandma started, "But…it hasn't been used since we came."

"That's fine." I abruptly left before my mom could utter a word.

I reached the broken down station within minutes. Hidden behind the elementary school and left untouched, the place really did look like a mess. Dead, leafless bushes bordered the sole platform. White paint was chipped and peeling off the ancient wood. I looked about. Why did I need to come here of all places?

I sighed and took out the train ticket. It was the first time I looked at it. I was to leave off of platform one, which seemed pointless to even state, promptly at noon. From there my next stop was a small wooden building. I looked at it again. A small wooden building? I never had a train *or* plane ticket before, but I sure knew that my destination couldn't be right.

Since I didn't have a watch on me and there wasn't a visible clock around, I didn't know the time. It seemed like five minutes passed before I heard something I thought I would never hear: a train whistle. It grew louder and louder and finally a small, one car train halted in front of me.

It was a bright and shiny blue, with a single red stripe going around just below the windows. The front looked like a traditional train, complete with a cow grill. A man, no taller than me, with a bushy moustache and large eyes hopped off. "Coming on?"

"I...don't know," I told him baffled.

"Ticket?" He eyed me curiously. I slowly stretched out my hand and he abruptly grabbed the ticket before I knew it. "Mhm," he muttered while scanning it. "Yup, you're coming on! Come on, come on, we don't have all day."

The conductor pushed me on board; I nearly tripped up the steps. The shades were pulled down, which gave the impression that the sun was setting on the horizon. As my eyes adjusted to the dull light, I realized the others on the train. No adults. Just a car of kids and teens. Why were they here? Were we all going to the small wooden building?

"Are you going to just stand there, or grab a seat?" the conductor politely questioned from behind me.

I jumped and looked swiftly behind me. I had forgotten all about him. Dilatorily, I took a timid step toward an empty seat next to a Hispanic girl who looked bored. She watched me the entire time, never stirring from her position. It gave me chills just knowing those golden orbs were following and overseeing my every move.

She flashed a smile at me. "Queta Lopez."

"Excuse me?" I asked, unsure.

She giggled. "My name. My name is Queta. Queta Lopez."

"Oh . . ." For the first time, I was unsure of what to say and found myself to be bashful, something I thought I'd never be. I saw her look at me, ushering me to tell my name as well. "Susan. Susan Lee."

"Hola Susan Lee. Why are you here?"

I sat there, stunned. Why was I here? What exactly could I tell her? I shrugged my shoulders and for the first time really looked at her. She didn't seem any older than me. Her hair was held in a bun with a Spanish comb. Three earrings per ear, with an ear cuff and a delicate chain that hooked from the first earring to the cuff. She wore a ring and bracelet and her jewelry was all silver, with a delicate and complicated design. Queta was definitely a girl who embraced everything about her heritage, and yet, she was still herself.

I hadn't realized the train had been moving until I saw a boy pull a window shade up. The scenery swept by as twilight was setting in. How long had I been on here? It only felt like five minutes, but had I really spent the entire afternoon on this train?

"Hungry?" Queta queried, offering me a bun.

Yet again, I swept my eyes around the car. Everybody was pulling out some sort of food: pizza, sushi, ravioli, baklava, and even poi. Where was this all coming from? And where did the conductor go?

"If you don't want the bun, you can have something else you know," the conductor said. I jumped and looked at him. He was standing beside me, looking at me curiously with a food cart. "But, perhaps what you need is to look out of your window," he added slyly before leaving through a door. Queta gave me a smile as she watched me frantically turn around and pull my shade up.

Water. All around us. A humpback whale passed by, as if it was normal to do this sort of thing. And then we were out. London. Paris. Berlin. Rome. Athens. Istanbul. Hong Kong. Seoul. Kyoto. They all went whizzing by. Landscapes changed, structures came and went, and yet the entire time I was amazed. There were people out there, millions of people all holding onto what they were. They knew what to embrace.

"It's pretty, isn't it?" Queta asked, staring out the window with me. I couldn't speak, I could just nod my head in agreement. "You said you didn't know why you were here, but I think I know why.

This train, you wouldn't have been able to ride it, much less see it, if you didn't even have an ounce of magic in you. Do you know why you're here now?"

"To figure out who I am…"

"That's right," she told me with a bright smile. "I hope you find what you're looking for."

As the sun began to rise, I began to notice a very familiar scene. Fields upon fields of never ending farmland continued to sweep by. On occasion I saw a horse, or a herd of cows, but mostly, in this small area of somewhere, it was mainly crops. And, as if right on cue, quaint buildings could be seen here and there fighting against the farmland. Slowly, slowly, more and more buildings popped up until we entered the edge of a small town. My heart began to race as Grandma's street came into view, and then her house. The house with just a slight touch of Oriental flair. The very house that I loved. Just as I turned back around, with Queta giving me a knowing look, I realized where this small wooden building was. Right where I began. The train station.

"I'm at the end of my journey, aren't I?" I questioned, looking at Queta with a forlorn look.

She gave me a bright smile. "If you have found what you are looking for, then yes, this is the end."

The conductor came out, gave me a nod, and opened the door.

I ran. I ran with everything I had. I ran across town. I ran up the winding driveway. I ran into the shop. I ran across all the planks. I ran through the cardboard boxes. I ran up the three flights of stairs. And I burst open the door, the smell of kimchi hitting my nose like a brick wall. "Great-Grandmother! Great-Grandmother! It was amazing!" I leaned behind the counter to find a man, opening a jar of kimchi.

"You mean the old lady? They don't live here anymore. Check in that old apartment," he grunted.

***

"Grandma?" I questioned timidly, as I went up the steps of the apartment.

"Susan! There you are! How have you been?" my mother asked when I opened the door.

"Where's Great-Grandmother? And why did they move? What's going on?"

Grandma came out of the kitchen. She seemed older than when I last saw her. A little of the spunk she had was gone from her step. "It was her dying wish to pass on to you her powers," she began slowly, setting the tea down onto the table.

I sat slowly down. "She's...dead?"

"Only those that mourn or are themselves dead wear white." There was a strain in her voice when she said it.

My mother took a sip of her tea before saying, "But, I know she's happy. She was always fond of you Susan." With that, I realized what I was. I came from a line of Koreans. But not only that, I was a witch. And for the first time in my life, I knew exactly what to embrace. Like Queta, I too would embrace my heritage, and yet, still stick to who I am.

I am Susan Lee, and no one can change that. No one.

This was another little flash fiction I wrote recently. I was stuck in my novel and really needed a change of pace before I decided to kill off all of my characters with a random nuclear explosion so that I wouldn't have to deal with them any longer. DeviantArt was having their annual April Fool's Day fun and the theme was Troll Face. One of their events for the day was to write a flash fiction with a troll. Frustrated with my own project, I decided to enter for the sheer fun of it. In the end, it helped me overcome my writer's block.

The Lonely Troll

Harry the troll peeked out from beneath his bridge. He didn't think it was fair that trolls had to live under bridges—wasn't this the 21st century after all?—but he continued to do so because that's what he was led to believe. Cars thundered overhead, causing him grievous migraines day in and day out. Oh, how he longed for the days when all he had to do was bask in the sun, awaiting for travelers to come across his bridge.

Back in those days when all the traveling had been by foot or horse, Harry had always jumped out. Sure he scared a few unsuspecting travelers, but he hadn't meant to. When people had come to his bridge he wanted to make sure that they were going in the right direction and were well rested enough. Most of the people were grateful, though there were a handful that had fled and insisted that he had wanted to eat them. That was disgusting! Why those people had spread that awful rumor about him, he would never know. Harry knew that trolls preferred to eat fresh fruit and berries. Meat—especially human meat—was vile.

When cars started to roll around, Harry was able to stop the occasional traveler to check on them, but now with GPS and cell phones, everyone ignored him and in the end he became more irritable with his frequent migraines and loneliness.

Gazing up at the flecks of dirt and rocks that came down with each passing car, Harry decided today was the day he was going to leave his bridge. With a big "Harumph!" he scooted away and began walking. He was only a few feet away when he looked back. His home had changed with the times, but regardless it was *his* bridge. The thundering and zipping was already relatively quieter here. He looked around. A person was further away, sitting beneath a tree.

Harry moved closer to the person. It was a male and he was engulfed in the paper in front of him. Feeling braver, Harry crept up behind the young man and took a peek at what it was that was so fascinating to this man. An epic battle ensued upon the page and the boy was feverishly placing lines here and there, turning it into a masterpiece. It was—undoubtedly—the most amazing thing Harry had ever seen. He wished he had the skills to come up with something like that, but he didn't because he was a troll.

"RARGH! STUPID!" Harry roared as a migraine seared through his skull.

The man jumped and turned around. He glared at Harry, marching away with his art.

Harry reached out to him, pleading. "Wait! I didn't mean—!" But it was too late. He was alone and always would be.

Going through some of my old work, I discovered some old school work. There was this fun, little project we were required to do in AP English that was one of the few creative writing projects we got to do. After having studied *The Canterbury Tales*, my English teacher thought it'd be great if we wrote two "tales" of our own. And on top of that we were required to read them in front of the class. Fun stuff, right? I was mortified and somehow managed to get through the reading, though I'm sure my face was red and I probably stuttered the entire time…

Again, not short stories, but I find the poems kind of humorous, so I'll share them with you.

Tale of the Drama Student

A drama student from high school
Was talking feverishly of a dual.
She was as pretty as a southern belle,
And in academics she did excel.
Her personality was quite bright,
But she always wanted to be quite right.
In a group she was over zealous,
But at times she seemed rather jealous.
That lead part was going to be hers,
If not hers, then to a man that slurs;
Singing songs from a 'a tale as old as time',
As she hums to Fleet Street to solve the crime.
Making pirouttes across the stage,
You wouldn't know her inner rage.
Although she was a triple threat,
She did not know about the set.
Her memory was quite great,
I'd think I'd call it top rate!
At the drop of a hat,
Shakespeare she could chat;
She had pearly whites,
And of average height,
Her gentle golden locks
Were as bright as her socks.
And that is my director's cut.

Tale of the Grandmother

There was with us a grandmother
Who hailed from eastern thither.
She wore a red and blue hanbok
To which the others grew to mock.
Her gentle eyes, to which deceived
Her strong desire for a male conceived.
A mirror hung from her plump waist,
Because she had such meticulous taste.
Her shiny hair was turning dull
Along with her laugh, like a cawing gull,
Were many of the things she wanted to change
If only her marriage wasn't arranged!
She's led a long hard life
Yet never complains of her strife;
Her face, hard as leather;
She smelled strongly of heather.
When it came to making decisions
There were always collisions;
It was either her way
Or the highway!
This tiny dragoness paid no heed
To the fact she wasn't of any need,
For in a society of patriarchs,
She indeed thought it matriarch!
But that is enough of that.

About the Author

A neek at heart, Sheenah Freitas has a love for the whimsical and magical. She looks to animated Disney movies and Studio Ghibli films for inspiration because of the innovative twists on fairytales, strong story structures, and character studies. When not writing, you might find her in a forest where she's yet to find any enchanted castles. You can learn more about her at her website at: www.sheenahfreitas.com.